WHIP HAND

Skye Fargo knew what Bullwhip Mulligan could do with his weapon of choice. The Trailsman had seen the corpse with its strips of skin flayed off, its face slashed to ribbons, its toes lopped off to bloody stumps.

Now he faced Mulligan, aching for revenge. The trouble was, Skye's hands were empty. Mulligan had his coiled whip in his.

Shaking it so that the long lash curled out, Mulligan rasped, "I was hopin' I'd get a crack at you, mister. Say your prayers."

Skye tried to dodge, but it was no use. The whip sizzled the air as it shot toward Fargo more swiftly than the human eye could follow. It caught him across the thigh. The pain was excruciating.

Mulligan sneered as Fargo futilely hobbled a few feet. "Hurt, did it? I've got news for you. It's just the beginning."

And the bullwhip hissed through the air again. . . .

**BE SURE TO READ THE OTHER
THRILLING NOVELS
IN THE EXCITING TRAILSMAN SERIES!**

DEVIL DANCE

by

FRANK BURLESON

The year 1858 dawns blood-red in the untamed Southwest, even as in the East the country moves toward civil war. Leadership of the most warlike Apache tribe has passed to the great warrior chief Cochise, who burns to avenge the poisoning of an Indian child. Meanwhile, the U.S. Army is out to end Apache power with terror instead of treaties.

As these two great fighting forces circle for the kill on a map stained by massacre and ambush, former dragoon officer Nathanial Barrington finds no escape from the clash of cultures he sought to flee. He is drawn west again to be tempted by a love as forbidden as it is irresistible—and to be torn between the military that formed him as a fighting man, and the hold the Apaches have on his heart and soul. . . .

Prices slightly higher in Canada   (18731-8—$5.99)

THE
TRAILSMAN
#183

BAYOU
BLOODBATH

by

Jon Sharpe

Ⓞ

A SIGNET BOOK

SIGNET
Published by the Penguin Group
Penguin Books USA Inc., 375 Hudson Street,
New York, New York 10014, U.S.A.
Penguin Books Ltd, 27 Wrights Lane,
London W8 5TZ, England
Penguin Books Australia Ltd,
Ringwood, Victoria, Australia
Penguin Books Canada Ltd, 10 Alcorn Avenue,
Toronto, Ontario, Canada M4V 3B2
Penguin Books (N.Z.) Ltd, 182-190 Wairau Road,
Auckland 10, New Zealand

Penguin Books Ltd, Registered Offices:
Harmondsworth, Middlesex, England

First published by Signet, an imprint of Dutton Signet,
a division of Penguin Books USA Inc.

First Printing, March, 1997
10 9 8 7 6 5 4 3 2

Copyright © Jon Sharpe, 1997
All rights reserved

The first chapter of this book originally appeared in *Blood Canyon*,
the one hundred eighty-second volume in this series.

Ⓣ REGISTERED TRADEMARK—MARCA REGISTRADA

Printed in Canada

The Trailsman

Beginnings . . . they bend the tree and they mark the man. Skye Fargo was born when he was eighteen. Terror was his midwife, vengeance his first cry. Killing spawned Skye Fargo, ruthless, cold-blooded murder. Out of the acrid smoke of gunpowder still hanging in the air, he rose, cried out a promise never forgotten.

The Trailsman they began to call him all across the West: searcher, scout, hunter, the man who could see where others only looked, his skills for hire but not his soul, the man who lived each day to the fullest, yet trailed each tomorrow. Skye Fargo, the Trailsman, and the seeker who could take the wildness of a land and the wanting of a woman and make them his own.

*Louisiana Bayou Territory, 1861,
where gators and cottonmouths were the
least of a man's worries. . . .*

1

The scream knifed through the muggy air like cold steel through human flesh.

It caused birds to take wing in startled flight. It spooked deer into bounding off into the brush. Even several alligators raised their heads to listen.

They were not the only ones.

A big man clad in buckskins reined up his pinto stallion and cocked his head to pinpoint the direction the scream came from. Piercing lake-blue eyes surveyed the bayou country that stretched before him. The winding wetlands, broken by dense tangles of vegetation, were home to many predators, both wild beasts and the two-legged kind. As the scream just proved, it did not do for anyone to let down their guard when traveling through southern Louisiana.

Skye Fargo loosened his Colt in its holster and kneed the Ovaro forward. The woman who voiced that cry had to be in dire trouble. Since he had never been one to turn his back on a lady in distress, he decided to find out what was going on and to help her if she needed it.

The Trailsman's instincts did not let him down. Sticking to solid ground, he wound deeper into the lush growth until he heard muffled voices ahead. Slowing, he passed through a stand of weeping willows and halted shy of a grassy area.

Four men surrounded a lovely brunette in a tight homespun dress. She was flat on her back, her green eyes wide with fear. Her fright seemed to strike them as humorous. One poked her with a boot, then laughed when she cringed. Another grabbed at her hair, but she jerked her head away.

"Is that any way to treat your old friend, Lacombe? After all the times I've been to your house, *chérie*?"

The man named Lacombe was tall and lanky. He wore dark pants, a dark shirt, and a black coat that hung clear down to his ankles. A shock of brown hair crowned his hawkish features. Bending, he hooked a finger under the woman's chin and blew a kiss at her.

"You do remember how friendly I tried to be, don't you, *ma petite*?"

Another man in shabby clothes slipped a grimy hand into a pocket and pulled out a length of rope. "What are we waitin' for, Henri? Let's get this over with. I ain't got all year." He reached for the woman's arm, but she cowered back. "Make it easy on yourself, wench, or we'll have to get rough."

Skye Fargo had seen enough. He spurred the pinto into the open, his right hand resting on the butt of his pistol. "I'm new to these parts, gents, but I know this isn't how most men in Louisiana treat pretty females. I'd back off if I were you."

The man with the rope stiffened. "Who the hell is he? What's he doing here?"

A third ruffian in a floppy hat took a few steps toward the stallion. He had a face that looked as if it had been sat on by a bear, and a Remington revolver tucked under his wide brown leather belt. "You picked the wrong place to be at the wrong time, mister. Turn that nag around and get going, or you'll regret it."

Fargo never had taken kindly to being threatened. Kneeing the pinto so it turned broadside to the scruffy gunman, he said, "It must be hard going through life as dumb as an ox. Makes a man wonder how you've lived as long as you have." He watched the ruffian's dark eyes. They would give him the telltale clue.

The gunman glanced at Henri Lacombe, who nodded. Smirking, the man then planted his feet wide, saying, "I'm not half as dumb as you, mister. At least I know better than to butt into things that are none of my affair." His hand lowered to within an inch of the Remington. "Any last words, busybody?"

"A few," Fargo said.

"Let's hear them."

Fargo had not taken his eyes off the gunman's. "Did you have any idea when you got up this morning that this was the last day of your life?" He saw anger flush the man scarlet, saw the slight tightening of the eyes that told him what the gunman was going to do.

They drew. The gunman must have fancied himself fast, but he had deluded himself. Fargo's Colt was out and leveled before the other man's pistol cleared leather. He had the hammer curled back before the barrel straightened and squeezed the trigger the instant it did.

The slug caught the gunman in the sternum, punching him backward. Tottering wildly, he crashed to earth at the feet of Henri Lacombe. No one else so much as twitched. Lacombe cracked a sly smile, then whistled in appreciation. "I thought I'd seen some fine shootin' in my time, *monsieur*. But you top everything."

Fargo cocked the Colt and pointed it at Lacombe. "I can do it again if you liked it so much. I can do it three more times, in fact."

The cutthroats with Lacombe exchanged worried looks.

Henri Lacombe chuckled. "*Homme d'esprit*, eh? No, that won't be necessary. We'll be going now. You've made your point." Raising his hands in mock surrender, he started to back off.

"You're putting the cart before the horse," Fargo said grimly. "I'm not done yet."

"How so?"

"Take off your boots and your pants."

Lacombe visibly tensed. His companions became more worried, one nervously licking his lips. "You can't be serious, *monsieur*. You'd make us walk all the way back half undressed? Through the *swamps*?"

Fargo shrugged. "Maybe it will teach you some manners. I wouldn't want to hear that you make a habit of pushing young women around. I'd have to look you up if I did. You wouldn't want that."

Unlike the gunman, Lacombe was too shrewd to let his feathers be ruffled. He smiled again, a devious twinkle in his gaze. "You and me, *homme*, we are a lot alike, I think."

"Shuck those boots and pants."

The other two hesitated, obeying only when Lacombe laughed and told them to comply. Fargo let them keep their underwear on, such as it was. The burliest of the cutthroats wore a pair that had not been washed in ten years, if that. The other had so many holes in his that there was not enough wool left to feed a starved moth. They glared at him the whole time they were undressing.

Henri Lacombe was different. He hummed to himself, neatly folded his pants, and set his shoes side by side. Straightening, he winked at the brunette. "How about this sight, *chérie*? Three half-naked men. What would your mother say?"

"Pick a direction and walk," Fargo commanded. Suddenly, the burly character clenched his fists and made as if to rush him. Feeling charitable, Fargo snapped a shot into the ground close to the man's dirty toes. "I'd think twice before I'd do that again," he advised.

Lacombe slapped his companion's shoulder. "Enough, Wilson! Are you tryin' to get us killed? We go while we can. There are always other days." Backing off, he gave a little wave. "I can't say it's been all that pleasant, *monsieur*, but I can say it has been educational. When next we meet, I will not take you lightly." Pivoting, he ambled off, whistling happily as if he did not have a care in the world. His sulking friends trailed along. Both cast longing looks at their boots and pants.

Fargo did not holster the Colt until they were out of sight. First he replaced the spent cartridge, and as he did, he noticed that the brunette had not moved. "Are you all right, ma'am?" he asked.

For some reason the simple question provoked a wellspring of tears. She sobbed once, then pushed erect and stood smoothing her wrinkled dress. "I thank you, sir, for helping me," she choked out. "It was awful kind of you." She paused to dab at her eyes. "Not that it will do any good. They'll get me in the long run. They always get the ones they're after."

"Who are they? Why do they want you?"

The brunette glanced at him, abject despair mirrored by her expression. She opened her lush mouth, as if to say more, but evidently changed her mind. Pressing a hand to her forehead, she gazed in the direction Lacombe and his friends had taken, then she spun to the southwest and bounded off like a frightened antelope.

"Wait!" Fargo called out. "You have nothing to be afraid of!"

It was a waste of breath. The woman was not about to stop. Her long legs flying, she weaved among the trees and bushes with the skill of someone who had lived in bayou country all her life. He caught a flash of silken thigh before she disappeared.

Fargo sighed and shook his head. The incident had been a hell of a way to start a new day. Clucking the pinto onward, he rode deeper into the swamp. For perhaps the hundredth time, he wondered if he wasn't making a fool of himself. He had come so far. What if it turned out to be someone's warped idea of a prank? Or a child's fantasy?

Fargo had been about to indulge in a week of wine, women, and wild times when the letter reached him. Flush with winnings from a stud poker game in Texas, he had decided to treat himself to some civilized hospitality and checked into his favorite hotel in St. Louis. The first order of business had been a hot bath in a big tub. He had been up to his neck in water and suds when the desk clerk timidly rapped on the door. "It's open," Fargo had hollered.

The mouse of a man came over holding a battered envelope. "I'm terribly sorry to bother you, sir, but the stage just came in, and this was in the mail pouch for you." He handed it over and got out of there, as if embarrassed to be in the same room with someone taking a bath.

Fargo had not known what to make of the envelope. It was addressed simply, SKYE FARGO, THE TRAILSMAN. The handwriting was the scrawl of a small child. Judging by the postmarks, the letter had been mailed from Baton Rouge to New Orleans. From there someone had sent it on to Denver. The rest were a jumble, but it appeared that the letter had followed him across the West, from Denver to Topeka, from Topeka to Forth Worth, from Fort Worth to St. Louis. It was a small miracle the thing ever caught up with him.

He had opened it, read the two sentences, and blurted, "What the hell?" The message had been short and to the point, in the same scrawl as that on the front of the envelope. "Mr. Trailsman," he read aloud. "My sister has been taken by bad men. Please come quick." The writer signed it, "Jessica Tanner, Possum Hollow."

Fargo had tossed the letter onto a dresser and not given it another thought. It had been ridiculous to think that he would saddle up and head off to somewhere he had never heard of just because a girl barely old enough to write claimed her sister was in trouble. He'd bathed and dressed, and gone across the street to a fancy restaurant where a sultry woman in a red dress had caught his eye.

For a while all had gone well. Fargo had introduced himself, and she had proven to be the friendly sort. After an expensive meal, they had gone off to a nearby theater. That was when the damn note kept popping into his head. He'd be staring at the actors on the stage and instead see the note in his mind's eye. He'd look at the woman, and there it was again. Try as he might—and did he ever try!—he could not stop thinking about it.

Jezebel had invited Fargo to her room after the play. He'd gladly gone, hoping that the delights he was about to savor would help him forget the little girl's appeal. Yet when Jezebel stood before him in all her naked glory, he had looked at her ample bosom and seen the child's hand-writing scrawled across her chest.

It had been too aggravating for words. He'd practically thrown Jezebel onto her bed and coupled with her with the ferocity of a wildcat. The scratch marks she had left had not healed for days.

At the crack of dawn Fargo had been at the stable to re-claim the Ovaro. He'd booked passage for himself and the horse on a steamboat heading south down the mighty Mississippi. On arriving in Baton Rouge, he had asked around and learned that Possum Hollow was the name of a tiny town in a remote part of the bayou.

Now here he was, enduring stifling heat and swarms of mosquitoes, always on the lookout for poisonous snakes and giant gators, wishing he was anywhere but where he was, and all because a child had pleaded for his aid. Sometimes he amazed himself.

It was interesting that the brunette had gone in the same direction he was headed. It might mean that Possum Hollow was not far ahead. No one in Baton Rouge had been able to tell him exactly how many miles he had to travel because no one he met in Baton Rouge had ever been to Possum Hollow. As a riverman had phrased it, "No one lives there but swamp trash, breeds, and bugs. Don't blink when you ride past, friend, or you'll miss it."

Lily pads and reeds appeared on the left. Fargo heard a bullfrog croak, another answer. The buzz of insects was a steady drone. In the grass to his right something rustled. He spied a sinuous form covered with scales, but it slithered off before he could get a good look at it. Which was just as well. The swamp crawled with cottonmouths, copperheads, and rattlesnakes. As if that were not enough, coral snakes were plentiful, too.

Having lived his whole life in the wilderness, Fargo knew all the wild creatures and their habits. He had learned to live with grizzlies, wolves, mountain lions, and wolverines. He tolerated skunks, buzzards, and coyotes. But he had never, ever been very fond of snakes. The truth was, they made his skin crawl. He'd as soon shoot one as look at it, although he never did unless the reptile posed a threat.

The terrain became more marshy. Swamp closed in on both sides until the strip of dry ground was no more than thirty feet wide. Fargo was about convinced that he would have to change course when he came on a well-marked trail. The number of hoofprints and footprints told him that the trail saw regular use. For over a mile he followed it, until all of a sudden he emerged from a stand of tall trees to find a narrow valley before him.

In the center was Possum Hollow. It consisted of seven shanty shacks made from uneven boards and mismatched scraps of lumber. Smoke wafted from a stovepipe jutting above the largest. A rutted excuse for a road wound among the buildings and vanished into the swampland on the far side.

The place was as quiet as a tomb. No one was about. The only living things Fargo saw were an old hog rooting around the base of a stump and a flock of chickens pecking at the dirt. He had a feeling, though, that unseen eyes were on him, that the residents of the sleepy hamlet knew he was there. How they knew, he couldn't say. Backwoods folks had their ways.

Fargo rode on, his right thumb wedged under his gun belt close to the Colt. A flicker of movement in the darkened doorway of the first shack drew his interest. He tensed, ready to draw, then grinned when a filthy, naked toddler waddled onto the rickety porch and gawked at him as if he were an apparition. The next second a woman in a tattered dress darted outside, grabbed her offspring around the waist, and scooted back inside.

Fargo had been to some out-of-the-way spots in his time. He had visited the heart of the Everglades, gone into the Appalachian hill country. In both regions it was not uncommon to meet people who would rather keep to themselves, who were naturally suspicious of any and all strangers.

Here it was different. He had a gut feeling that there was more to the absence of the inhabitants than was apparent. The fleeting glance the mother had thrown at him had been a fearful one, almost as if she dreaded that he would do her harm.

The short hairs at the nape of Fargo's neck prickled as he entered the pitiful excuse for a town. He passed a darkened window and thought he saw a vague figure staring at him. From one of the dwellings came the voice of an older child that was punctuated by a slap. He drew rein at a rickety hitching post in front of the large building. The creak of his saddle as he swung down seemed eerily loud.

Looping the reins, Fargo walked around the rail onto the plank post. On the side of the building a mule and two horses were tied. Near the door, painted in crude letters, was a sign: BIG BOB'S LIQUOR, TACK AND EMPORIUM. Fargo doubted that the man who wrote it even knew what an emporium was, since that word and half the others were misspelled.

The door hung open. Fargo stepped inside, promptly stepping to the right so his back was to the wall. The interior was dim, the only source of light the sunlight streaming in through a window and the doorway. Two tables and chairs filled the middle of the floor. On one side was a counter, on the other a stove on which a pot of coffee perked. Shelves lined all the walls, most crammed with dusty merchandise.

Guessing who was known as Big Bob was not hard. A man the size of a mountain lounged against the counter. A

17

dirty apron hung around his ample waist. Flesh, jowls and flabby arms quivered when he moved, as if he were made of pudding and not flesh and blood. Regarding Fargo coldly, he said, "Howdy, stranger. We don't get many pilgrims passing through these parts."

Fargo was studying the other two. They were brothers, one a few years older than the other, but so alike in their scarecrow frames, unkempt black hair, and faded homespun clothes that there was no mistaking the resemblance. The older one had a butcher knife in a hip sheath and a Sharps rifle held in the crook of an elbow. His brother was partial to a Bowie knife and a pistol worn butt forward on the left hip. They met his stare, and theirs was not friendly.

"What will it be?" Big Bob asked. "I've got whiskey and ale." He moved behind the counter. "If you think you can handle it, I've also got some local brew that would grow hair on a bald man."

The brothers snickered at Bob's little joke. Fargo crossed to the counter, positioning himself so that he could keep one eye on the door and the other on Bob and his customers. Through the window he could see the Ovaro. "A glass of whiskey will wash down the dust," he said.

"Coming right up." Big Bob had to stoop to reach under the counter. Selecting a glass, he wiped it with his apron, filled it halfway, and brought the glass over. "That'll be a dollar."

"For one drink?" Fargo said.

Big Bob jabbed a thick thumb at the assorted bottles lining a shelf. "Do you think I get this stuff brought in from Baton Rouge for free? They charge me extra if they bring it themselves, so twice a year I have to go up there with a pack horse and tote back a couple of cases."

Fargo swallowed, savoring the burning sensation that scorched his throat and stomach. At least the whiskey was not watered down. Fishing in his pocket, he removed two gold quarter eagles and slapped them on the wood.

Bob's bushy eyebrows puckered. "You must want a whole bottle."

"I want information." Fargo set him straight. "You can keep the change if you can help me out." He took another sip. "I need directions to the Tanner place."

Something happened. Fargo detected a change in the three men, a barely noticeable tensing, and in Bob's case a twitching of those heavy jowls. The brothers whispered, then stared at him more coldly than ever. "I know the Tanners live around here. You must know them."

"Can't say as I do," Big Bob said. He turned. "How about you two boys? You've lived in these parts all your lives. Ever heard tell of a family by that name?"

The older brother answered. "Can't rightly say as we have. What's your business with them, anyway, mister?"

"It's *my* business," Fargo stressed. Polishing off his drink, he picked up the eagles and slapped a dollar on the counter in their place. "No information, no tip."

Big Bob stared wistfully at the pocket the gold eagles had gone into. "We didn't mean to rile you none, stranger. These boys are the Genritt brothers, Buck and Morco. If Buck says he's never heard of them, then someone must have sent you on a wild-goose chase."

It was so obvious that they were lying that Fargo was tempted to force them to tell the truth. But the other locals might not take too kindly to having some of their own pistol whipped. Walking outdoors, he surveyed Possum Hollow. The chickens were gone, leaving the street all to the hog. It ambled toward him, grunting noisily, maybe hoping for a handout.

Unhitching the Ovaro, Fargo led it to the next building. The door was closed, so he knocked. Footsteps scraped within, and there were muted voices. No one, though, responded to his knock. He tried again with the same result. Whoever was inside wanted nothing to do with him.

Five shacks were left. Fargo walked to the next. Flowers

had been planted under a window covered by burlap. Through a crack an eyeball peeked out at him. He pretended not to see it and halted in front of a door someone had left cracked open. "Hello?" he said. "I'd like a word with you, if you don't mind."

The same pattern repeated itself. Feet pattered. Muttering broke out. Fargo rapped his knuckles on the jamb. "I don't mean any harm. I'd just like some information. Please. Open the door."

His request was granted, but not in the manner Fargo expected. The door was abruptly flung wide, and he found himself looking down the barrel of a cocked rifle.

2

It was an old flintlock, a Kentucky rifle, a type rarely seen anymore. Though remarkably accurate at long distances, they had been prone to misfire. So much so, that "a flash in the pan" became a common saying when people talked about someone who talked big but did little.

Fargo was not about to gamble that the rifle held by the woman glaring at him would not discharge as it should. She was a sturdily built matron with streaks of gray in her hair and a definite streak of meanness in her eyes. Her dress had been store-bought ages ago. Her skin had that weathered look of a person who worked long and hard. A square jaw hinted at iron character. She arched a gray-flecked eyebrow and raked him with a look of sheer contempt.

"I'm tellin' you right now, mister, that you ain't gettin' my girl. Lay a finger on her and I'll put a hole in you the size of a melon."

"You don't—" Fargo tried to explain, and was jabbed in the chin by the muzzle.

"What I don't want is to hear your lies, vermin. Just get out of here before I forget that I'm a lady. Don't ever let me see you within fifty feet of my home ever again. Now get."

Fargo did the smart thing and backed away, holding his hands out to show that he was not looking for trouble. When she lowered the Kentucky slightly, he made bold to say, "All I wanted was directions to the Tanner place."

"Haven't your kind done them enough hurt?" the woman snapped. "You leave Constance and her girls be."

Another woman unexpectedly appeared behind her. This one was barely out of her twenties, a beauty with raven hair and eyes to match, her homemade dress clinging to her supple form as if designed to mold to her shapely contours. She looked at Fargo and seemed about to speak. Then she glanced at the older woman and faded into the murky background without uttering a word.

Once Fargo was in the street, the door slammed shut. Not about to give up, he walked to the next shack. Thanks to the matron, he now knew that there was indeed a family called the Tanners. After traveling so far to find them, he was more determined than ever to look up little Jessica.

But the occupants of the last three buildings proved to be of no help. No one would even come to the door. Thwarted, Fargo stepped into the stirrups and rode out of Possum Hollow along a winding trail that was bound to bring him to a homestead sooner or later.

Fargo had met some unfriendly folks in his time, but it was safe to say that he'd never been to a town where everyone treated him as if he were pond scum or had the plague, or both. He tried to figure out why, but he lacked too many pieces of the puzzle. All he could say for sure was that it would be wise to approach any cabins he came across with his hands nowhere near his hardware. The homesteaders were liable to shoot first and ask him what he was doing there later.

Almost immediately trees and undergrowth hemmed in the trail on both sides. Sparrows frolicked in the branches. Butterflies flitted about. Fargo checked over a shoulder but saw no one shadowing him. As he faced around, a twig crunched off to the left. The sparrows took wing.

He pretended not to have noticed and took off his hat. Making a show of mopping his brow with his sleeve, Fargo lowered the hat to his right side, covering the Colt so he could draw it without being seen. A bend appeared. He cocked his pistol as he went around the turn.

In the middle of the trail stood the raven-haired beauty from the second shack. In the sunlight she was more dazzling, her hair lustrous and long, her complexion a healthy bronze, the swell of her chest and her thighs as enticing as a juicy steak would be to a man who was half-starved. Surprisingly, she wore no shoes. Her feet were dainty and clean.

Fargo reined up, replacing his hat. She did not show any fear at the sight of the cocked Colt. "I was just being careful," he said, afraid she would run off. Letting down the hammer, he twirled the six-shooter into its holster. The beauty offered no comment. "What can I do for you?"

"What's your business with the Tanners, mister?" she asked bluntly. Her voice was a throaty purr, the kind that jangled a man to his core, that put visions in his head of silken sheets and soft down mattresses and all-night bouts of wild passion.

Fargo hesitated. Could he trust her? Was she a friend of theirs or did she have another reason for asking? "Mind telling me why you're so curious?"

"I'd like to, but I ain't so sure I can trust you," the woman responded. "Lacombe don't take kindly to meddlers. That crafty Cajun has spared me so far, and I'd like to keep it that way."

Lacombe again. Fargo keenly regretted letting those three men walk off. He should have demanded to know what they were up to or quizzed the woman they had been molesting. "I've met the gent. Can't say as I think highly of him." He paused. "What's your name, by the way?"

"Desma Collinder. That was my ma who ran you off with her gun back yonder. Don't hold it against her. She was just lookin' out for me." Desma studied him like a hawk studying its quarry. "You're him, aren't you? The one who gets writ up in the papers, the one folks talk about so much? The one they call the Trailsman?"

Fargo nodded.

"Well, I'll be!" Desma exclaimed, brightening. "I figured Jessie was wastin' her time. I told her that an important person like you had better things to do than go gallivantin' across the country just because some little girl wrote you a letter." She scrutinized his face. "You're a lot younger than I figured you would be. A heap better lookin', too."

Country girls! Fargo reflected wryly. They had a flair for being frank and brazen, for saying what they pleased as it suited them. This one was like a ripe fruit ready to burst. It made his mouth water to look at her. "One compliment deserves another. If you don't mind my saying so, you must be the prettiest woman in these parts."

Desma Collinder blushed nicely. Clasping her hands behind her back, she fidgeted, saying, "Shucks. I'm not nothin' special. You should have seen Jessie's older sister, Jasmine. Now, there was a girl who could turn a man's head so fast, his neck would break."

She smiled, and Fargo did the same. At last he had met someone who could explain why Possum Hollow was in the grip of so much fear and hatred. Then she gazed past him and went as rigid as a board. To his consternation, she spun and bolted into the vegetation, bounding like a terrified doe, moving faster in her bare feet than most could have done in shoes or boots. Suspecting that her mother had caught them, Fargo twisted.

It was the Genritt brothers. They had snuck up on him while he was distracted by Desma. The older one, Buck, had him covered with the Sharps.

"What do you two want?" Fargo blustered.

Buck steadied the heavy-caliber rifle on his chest. "I'd be civil if I were you. You're in enough trouble as it is, stranger."

"That's right," Morco sneered. "We don't like it when people start nosin' around things that have nothin' to do with them. We reckon that someone should learn you some manners."

"And you think that you're the men to do it?" Fargo said, tensing to make his move should the Hawken waver.

"We're handy," Buck said. "Now, climb down from there before I get a notion to put windows in your skull."

Fargo had no choice. They had him dead to rights. Having once owned a Sharps, he was well aware what a slug from one could do. Moving slowly in order not to provoke the older Genritt into firing, he swung from the saddle and released the reins. The younger brother swaggered forward, careful not to get in Buck's line of fire.

"We saw you with Desma," Morco declared. "What was she doin' here? What were the two of you talkin' about?"

Fargo shrugged. "We were passing the time of day." No sooner were the words out of his mouth than he was slammed in the gut by an anvil. Or that's how it felt. Morco had drawn the Remington and driven the barrel into his abdomen in the blink of an eye. Acute agony seared through him. He gasped for breath and saw Morco help himself to the Colt.

"We want the truth, stranger," Buck warned. "Give us any trouble and I'll let my brother do as he pleases. That would be a mistake on your part. I once saw him flay the skin off a lousy injun just because the buck had the gall to cross our property without askin' permission."

Morco threw the Colt into the grass, then drew his Bowie. "That gives me a brainstorm, big brother. How about if I skin this varmint alive and make a coin pouch out of his hide? We could give it to Ma for her birthday. Wouldn't that tickle her fancy!"

The younger brother looked back at the older one, and they both cackled. For an instant neither was watching Fargo. He seized that moment and sprang in front of Morco so Buck could not fire. Morco, still cackling, began to turn toward him, and Fargo hit him, a jarring blow to the jaw that rocked Morco on his heels. The Remington went flying. Taking a step, Fargo tackled Morco around the waist.

They fell locked together, but as they landed, Fargo pushed off into a roll that brought him to his feet next to Buck, who was so stunned by the sudden turn of events that he stood there flat-footed.

Fargo delivered a solid punch to the midsection, another to the cheek. Buck folded up on himself, falling to his knees and sputtering. Fargo drew back a foot to kick him in the head. The next second a runaway steam engine plowed into his back and hurled him to the ground. He heard a shriek of rage, felt Morco's fists pounding his head and shoulders. Flipping to the right, Fargo dislodged him.

Buck was already rising. Fargo caught the older Genritt with a powerful right to the ear that toppled him like a poled ox. Shifting, Fargo barely had time to set himself before Morco waded in again, raining punches in random fury. Fargo blocked most of them. One clipped his chin, another his brow. He ducked a wicked uppercut, dodged a kick to the groin, then slipped in close and struck Morco in the throat.

Gurgling noisily, turning red in the face, Morco clutched himself and staggered backward.

Fargo wanted to finish Morco then and there. But Buck came to his brother's rescue, catching him around the ankles and bearing him down. They grappled, Buck striving to clamp his hands on Fargo's throat, Fargo holding Buck at bay until he could get his legs up and shove, pushing Buck off him. The two of them scrambled up into a crouch. Buck swung, but Fargo countered and flicked a right cross that sent Buck stumbling toward the trees.

The gleam of sunlight off metal caught Fargo's eye. He glanced down and spied the Colt. Throwing himself at it, he palmed the smooth grips and rotated.

The Genritt brothers were gone. Just like that, they had disappeared in the heavy growth. Fargo listened, but there was no crackling of brush, no rustling of leaves. Nor would there be. Buck and Morco had been born and bred in the bayou country. They were more at home in the swamps than they would be in a big city. They were not about to give themselves away.

Rising, Fargo went to the Ovaro. Along the way he helped himself to the Sharps and the Remington. Leaving them there invited a shot in the back. He stuck them into his bedroll, climbed on, and continued westward, not replacing the Colt until he had gone over a mile.

Desma Collinder did not show herself again. The untimely interruption had spoiled the best and only opportunity Fargo had so far to get to the bottom of the mystery. He stayed alert as the valley narrowed, uncharted swampland covering wide areas. A whiff of smoke let him know that somewhere nearby was a fire. The whiff brought with it the tantalizing aroma of food. He trotted along a series of curves that brought him to a tilled field and a rickety cabin. The smoke curled from a stone chimney.

"Anyone home?" Fargo called out.

Chickens were present again. So were several pigs in a muddy pen. They poked their pink snouts between the uneven rails and grunted as Fargo crossed to a wide porch.

"I need some directions."

Just like in Possum Hollow, no one bothered to reply. Inside, a dog growled. A big dog, by the sound of it, the kind that would tear into an intruder and not stop tearing until it or the intruder was dead. Someone told it to shush, and it did.

Fargo could take a hint. He rode on, skirting the corn to where a narrow trail bore steadily deeper into the heart of the bayou. As the foliage closed in around him again, he cast a glance at the cabin and spotted a man staring at him from a window. A shotgun barrel was visible. Fargo was glad he had not knocked on the door. He probably would have been met with a load of buckshot.

The heat climbed, the humidity worsened. Fargo's shirt clung to his back. He would have liked to take off his boots and dip his feet in a pool of cool water, but he did not have the time to spare.

About an hour after finding the cabin, Fargo came to a clearing. It had all the earmarks of being the handiwork of someone with an ax. So there must be another homestead near at hand. He was halfway across when his left arm flared with stinging pain. Automatically he drew the Colt and turned, thinking that he had been shot. Only no gunshot rang out. He looked at his arm but saw no tear in the buckskin, nor any blood.

"What the—?"

There was a whizzing sound. From out of nowhere flew a rock the size of a grape. It caught Fargo high in the shoulder, stinging worse than the first one had, and thudded to the ground. Someone was throwing stones at him! He scanned the woods for the culprit and spied a small shape back among the trees. It was a child, ten years old or so, with short brown hair, baggy clothes, and no footwear.

Fargo almost laughed at how ridiculous his quest was turning out. From being treated as if he were a rabid wolf, to having to fight for his life, to this. "Hold on there, sprout!" he hollered. "I'm not out to hurt you."

The boy raised an arm and swung a long leather thong overhead. The swish the sling made cleaving the air could be heard in the clearing. "Hold on!" Fargo repeated, reining toward the trees. "I'd like to talk to you if you can spare me a minute."

"Go away, bad man!" the child cried in a high-pitched voice. "Go away or I'll put your eye out!"

"Please—" Fargo said. That was as far as he got. The boy let fly. The stone was a brown streak against the backdrop of green as it flew true to the mark. Fargo bent, but he was not quite fast enough. Lancing agony shot through him when the stone caught him high in the forehead. His vision danced, his senses reeled. He had to grip the saddle horn to keep from falling.

"Go away!" the child insisted, quickly taking another stone from a pouch slung across his chest.

Fargo's patience had been frayed by his reception in Possum Hollow, then stretched to the breaking point, thanks to the treatment by the Genritt brothers. He was in no mood to abide more harsh treatment, even at the hands of a child. Kneeing the pinto into a lope, he threaded through the trees.

The boy ran. As fleet as an antelope, he bounded through the woodland as if born with wings on his feet. But as fleet as he was, he was still only human. He had no prayer of outrunning a horse.

The Ovaro began to gain. Fargo leaned low, his arm outstretched, intent on catching the youngster without hurting him. They sped into the open. The child appeared to have a destination in mind and made a beeline across a field. In doing so he enabled Fargo to bring the pinto to a gallop.

In no time Fargo was on top of the boy, his fingers closing on the back of the boy's shirt. He yanked, pulling the child off his feet and across the saddle so swiftly that the boy could not resist. Once caught, the youngster kicked and thrashed, screaming at the top of his lungs.

"Let me go! Let me go! My ma will kill you for this! You're mean, mean, mean!"

"Calm down," Fargo said as he gradually slowed the Ovaro. "I'm not going to lay a hand on you."

"You already have! Mean! Mean!"

Tiny hands slapped at Fargo's stomach and legs, but they inflicted no more pain than a mosquito bite. Still holding the boy by the scruff of the neck, he slid off and turned the fiercely struggling wildcat so they were eye to eye. "What got into you back there? You could have blinded me."

The child tried to kick him. "I'll blind you, all right! I'll blind all of you! Bring her back or I'll hunt all of you down when I get older and make you pay! I swear I will!"

Fargo flinched when the boy scraped his wrist with sharp fingernails. "If I let you go, do you give me your word not to run off? I need some help."

"I'll never help the likes of you!" the boy screamed, raining feeble backhands on Fargo's ribs. "Never, ever! I'd rather dunk you in quicksand! Or stick your head in a gator's mouth!"

A kick to the kneecap caught Fargo off guard. Pain pulsed up his leg. He had to grit his teeth to keep from using the kind of language he reserved for belligerent saloon rowdies and card cheats. "Now, simmer down!" he commanded, giving the boy a shake that rattled the child's teeth. "All I ask is that you listen to me."

A pistol blasted, so close that it caused Fargo to jump and spin as dirt spewed onto his boot. His right hand swooped to the Colt, but he checked his draw when he saw who had fired.

Ten feet away stood a middle-aged woman whose threadbare dress had seen better days years ago. She held an old Dragoon pistol in both hands, the set of her jaw leaving little doubt that she would fire again if she had to, the fire in her gaze proof that the next time she would not aim low. "Release my daughter," she directed, "or so help me, I'll kill you."

"Daughter?" Fargo said, genuinely amazed. He did not protest when the freed girl kicked him once more for good measure on the shin. "I'm sorry. I didn't know."

"Shoot him, Ma!" the girl crowed. "Fill him with lead! Show them that they can't keep doing this to us! Shoot him! Shoot him!"

The mother bit her lower lip, then said, "I should, you know, mister. You can't keep on terrorizin' folks like you do." She grew sorrowful. "I should have shot your boss the last time he came, but I couldn't bring myself to do it. Look at what it cost me!"

Fargo did not like how her forefinger kept stroking the

trigger. "I don't have a boss," he said hastily. "I'm not who you think I—"

The girl shook a fist at him. "Don't believe the lyin' polecat, Ma! Put a bullet smack between his eyes! Then we'll tie him to his horse and send him back to Lacombe."

"Hush, girl," the mother said. "I can't hardly think straight with all your jabberin'."

"But, Ma!" the peewee hellion wailed. "You know what they did to sissy! How can we let this mean man go on livin'? Why, in another five or six years they'll be comin' for me. Do you want to lose me, too?"

The mother was so distraught that she might accidentally fire. Fargo had seen it happen before. Motioning, he suggested, "Why don't the two of you calm down so we can talk this over? All I want is information, and I'll gladly be on my way and leave you in peace."

The girl pranced around her mother, tugging at the mother's dress. "Don't listen to him, Ma! He'd say anything to save his hide. Just shoot him and be done with it. Or march him down to the swamp and let Old Broken Tooth have him. That way no one can blame us."

"Listen," Fargo attempted to get a word in. He was silenced by a wag of the Dragoon.

"You've given me an idea, girl," the mother said. Stepping to the left, she pointed her heavy revolver at Fargo's head. "Fetch his gun, child. And, mister, if you so much as sneeze, you're a dead man."

Giggling gleefully, the girl circled around and slipped the Colt out. "I have it!" she cried, staying out of his reach as she carried her prize to the woman.

Now armed with both pistols, the mother became more confident. Nodding to the west, she said, "Walk that way. Don't stop until I tell you to."

A footpath linked the field to a homestead. A cabin sat to the north, a one-eyed cat sunning itself on the porch. A cow with a bell around its neck grazed nearby. In a small coop at the side of the cabin was a chicken coop. The woman had Fargo walk on another hundred yards, to a dank stretch of swamp. On the bank of a large pool, she ordered him to stop.

"Where's my oldest daughter, mister?"

"If I knew, I'd tell you," Fargo assured her.

The girl shook a finger at him. "Liar, liar, pants on fire!"

Her mother nodded at the pool. "Wade on in there." To accent her demand, she thumbed back the hammer of the Colt and pointed it at him as well.

Fargo complied, buying time so he could set her straight on who he was and his search for the Tanners. Descending a short, slippery slope, he entered the water. It was brackish and tepid, but it still felt good on his sweaty feet and legs. He stopped and turned. "All right. What now, lady?"

"Where's my daughter?"

"How many times do I have to tell you? I don't know."

The mother frowned. "I wish you would be honest with me. You only have yourself to blame for what happens next."

Suddenly the water in the center of the pool roiled, churned by something underneath. Fargo swung around just as a gigantic reptilian form broke the surface. His blood turned to ice. He backed toward the slope, losing his balance when his left foot slipped. The water rose as high as his chest before he caught himself. By then the creature in the middle had started toward him.

Old Broken Tooth, the girl had called it. The biggest alligator that Fargo had ever seen.

3

"This is your last chance, mister!" the woman cried. "Tell me what Lacombe did with my daughter or I'll let that gator tear you to shreds!"

Skye Fargo wanted to oblige her. The Cajun was his enemy as much as the Cajun was hers. Yet he could not reveal information he did not have. Slowly straightening, he retreated toward the bank, willing to risk being shot rather than confront the gator.

Alligators infested the cypress swamps and lowland bayous that stretched from Louisiana to Florida. They were a constant menace, killing many poor souls each year. Growing to a length of twenty feet, they were the lords of their domain. Though they roamed freely, quite often they picked certain ponds or pools as their home and defended their territory savagely.

This one swam slowly toward Fargo, its broad, round snout barely creating a ripple, its unblinking eyes fixed on him as it would fix them on any prey.

Fargo neared the slope. He was about to step out when the Dragoon thundered, kicking up mud inches from his leg.

"No you don't!" the mother railed. "I'm not lettin' you out of there until you tell me what I need to know!"

The gator edged closer. It opened its gaping maw, revealing that one of its larger teeth had broken off at one time and never been replaced by another.

Fargo had a decision to make. Either he stood there and let the beast attack him, his only weapon the slender throwing knife he secreted in an ankle sheath under his right boot, or he called the woman's bluff. The alligator's razor teeth and massive bulk were the deciding factors. Armed with just a knife, he would be dead in no time.

Squaring his shoulders, Fargo stared at the mother and marched up out of the pool. She recoiled, but not from fright. She acted astounded that he had defied her. Both pistols swung toward his chest, and her arms trembled as she snarled at him.

"For the last time, get back in there!"

"No."

The little girl was beside herself with anger. "Shoot him, Ma! Kill him for what they did! Make him pay, Ma! Do it! Now!"

Fargo locked his eyes on the mother's. "If you don't mind having the death of an innocent man on your conscience, then do as she wants." He was halfway up the bank. Old Broken Tooth had halted when he strode from the water and now closed its mouth. "I never laid a hand on your oldest daughter. I don't even know her." Fargo gained the top and straightened, his face a hand's width from the muzzles of the two revolvers. Her trigger fingers were twitching violently. "All I'm trying to do is find a family called the Tanners."

The mother's mouth imitated the gator's. "Who?"

"Tanners," Fargo repeated. "Don't tell me you've never heard of them. I know they live in this part of the bayou, and I aim to find them. So if you know where they are, I would appreciate directions." Fishing in his pocket, he produced the letter. "This was sent to me by their little girl—"

It hit him, then. When he said the word "girl," he knew. He stared at the tyke, who had been thirsting for his blood and held out the letter so she could see the handwriting and the signature. "You sent this, didn't you? You're Jessie Tanner."

Mother and child were stupefied. For practically a full

minute neither of them spoke. Then the girl nodded and took the letter from him, her hands shaking as badly as her mother's had just been. "You're him?" she said in a weak, awed voice. "You're the Trailsman?"

"I am."

"Oh, my God!" The outcry was torn from the mother's throat, a cry of mingled horror and despair. She swayed as if she might faint. "To think that I almost shot you!"

"Not to mention the gator," Fargo reminded her.

The woman made an offhanded gesture at the pool. "Broken Tooth is harmless. We feed him table scraps from time to time. That's why he swam up to you and opened his mouth. But he would never bite."

Fargo took small comfort from the news. Gators were notoriously temperamental. Like pet bears, they would turn on anyone who befriended them with no warning whatsoever. All would go well for days or weeks or even years, until one time the animals lashed out in a fit of bestial fury.

"If I had shot you, that would make me as bad as Lacombe and his crowd," the mother was saying. Aghast, she looked at the pistols. "Is that what they've brought me to? Have they pulled me down to their level?"

Fargo held out his hand, and she gave him the Colt. Walking on past them, he made for the clearing where he had left the Ovaro. He did not like leaving the stallion unattended.

"Wait!" the mother said. "You're not leaving, are you? Please don't! I can explain." Dashing up, she clasped his hand. "Please! I'm so sorry for what I've done. I mistook you for one of Lacombe's men. He's the rogue who took my Jasmine. Everyone suspects that he is to blame for all the disappearances."

Fargo had not slackened his pace. She fell into step beside him and Jessica did likewise on his other side. They were subdued, rendered timid by their blunder, afraid to meet his gaze. "I won't hold this against you, Mrs. Tanner," he said to put them at ease. "Maybe if I were in your shoes, I'd do the same thing."

Jessica was holding the letter as if it were the Holy Grail. "You're him!" she breathed. "I told everyone you'd come, and you did!"

The mother forced a smile. "Where are my manners? I'm Constance Tanner, but you can call me Connie." She paused. "My husband, George, died five years ago. He was out clearin' that field yonder when a snake bit him. Never did see what kind it was, but he died that evenin'."

"And you stayed on?" Fargo was mildly surprised. Eking out a living in the swamp country was hard enough for a couple. A lone woman, saddled with children, was in for more hardships than most could endure.

"I know what you're thinkin'," Constance said. "But I couldn't see movin' to the big city and livin' in a cramped apartment. I'd be lucky to get a job, and those I could get wouldn't hardly pay enough for the three of us to live off of." She gazed fondly at the cabin. "It's not much, our place, but here my girls can roam as they please. We have plenty of fresh eggs and milk. My girls keep meat on the table. They're both wizards with slingshots—"

"So I learned," Fargo said.

Connie's smile this time was for real. "I am sorry about that. Jessie gets carried away sometimes."

"I'm sorry, too," the girl chimed in.

The mother changed the subject. "Can you blame me for not leavin'? I'd never be able to find a buyer for our place. Few want to live out this far, and those that do just pick a parcel of empty land and settle." She indicated a vegetable garden behind the cabin. "I'd hate to see all the work George and I put into our home go to waste."

"You don't need to justify your actions to me," Fargo said. "But it would help if you told me about Jasmine and Lacombe."

Constance's features clouded. "He's a slick one, that

devil. He showed up in these parts about a year ago. He'd come and go, sometimes to Baton Rouge, sometimes elsewhere. No one made the connection at first, but that's when the girls started to disappear."

"How many has it been?"

"Eight. My Jasmine was the last. It's always the prettiest ones. Always the ones that Lacombe has taken a shine to." Constance clenched her fist. "Him with his big-city ways, his glib tongue, and all that money he flashes around. Small wonder the girls fall for him."

They drew within sight of the field. Fargo looked but did not see the stallion. It must have wondered off, he reasoned, and scoured the woods beyond.

"I tried to warn Jasmine," Constance had gone on. "I told her what me and a bunch of the other mothers suspected, but would she listen? I should say not! All that mattered to her was that handsome Henri Lacombe had bought her a new dress and a new comb and kept comin' around and fillin' her head with talk of how wonderful she was."

"Did you see him take her away?"

The mother growled like a dog about to bite. "Of course not. Do you think he's stupid? Jessie and me went off to pick berries, and when we got back Jasmine was gone. She'd left a note sayin' that she wanted to be on her own and not to hunt for her. But it just wasn't like her. That girl loved to give me sass. She would have told me to my face."

Fargo had yet to spy the Ovaro. He was growing more concerned by the second, but he thought to ask, "Did the other missing girls leave notes, too?"

"As far as I know, yes."

"Did any of the notes mention Lacombe?"

"Nary a one."

Fargo had to hand it to the Cajun. Whatever Lacombe was up to, he covered his tracks well. Should the families of the missing women go to the sheriff, there was no proof linking him to the disappearances. He inquired about that.

Connie Tanner snorted. "Go to the law? Mister, the nearest law officers are in Baton Rouge. Do you honestly think they give a hoot about what happens out here in the sticks? Why, they don't even come out here when there has been a killin'." She glowered at the world in general. "Big Bob likes to make on that he's the law in these parts, but he's only the justice of the peace. The mother of one of the missing girls went to see him about it. He patted her hand and told her that she had nothin' to worry about, that he'd look into it and fetch her girl back in no time. What a crock!"

Fargo reached the exact spot where he had left the pinto. The tracks revealed the stallion's fate. He drew the Colt and checked whether any cartridges needed to be replaced.

Suddenly alarmed, Connie asked, "What are you doing?"

"Going after my horse. The Genritt brothers stole it." Fargo headed for the trees. "Don't worry. I'll be back, and then we'll find out where Jasmine is. Lacombe has a lot to answer for."

Jessica tugged at the fringe on his buckskin pants. "Hold on, Mr. Fargo. We know where the Genritt's live. I can show you a shortcut that will get you there before them."

Fargo was tempted, but it would be rash to expose the child to possible harm. "Thanks for the offer, but it's best if you stay with your mother."

"Then I'll guide you," said a sultry voice from out of the bushes, and into the sunlight stepped Desma Collinder.

"Desma!" Jessie squealed, throwing herself at her friend in sheer delight. "Where did you come from? We weren't expectin' you until Saturday."

Desma had not taken her eyes off Fargo. "I was followin' the Genritt brothers. They've got eyes like hawks, so I had to stay far back or I would have seen what they were up to and yelled to warn you."

Connie was as pleased to see their friend as her daughter. "Come inside and have a cup of tea, my dear. Then you can go after the Genritts. I want to hear how your ma is doing and whether that awful Cajun is still pesterin' you."

"That will have to wait," Desma said. "Mr. Fargo's horse is more important. You know as well as I do that those Genritts might carve it up for their supper."

Fargo had figured that the brothers took the stallion to keep or to sell. Having ridden it for so long, he was almost as attached to the pinto as Constance Tanner was to her girls. The thought of someone eating it churned his stomach. "Let's go," he said gruffly, hurrying on.

The tracks did not stick to the trail. They veered to the south, the footprints showing that one of the brothers had pulled on the reins while the other walked behind to swat the stallion when it slowed. Which the Ovaro did often. It did not like being handled by someone it did not know.

Desma caught up, caught at his sleeve. "Hold on. I can understand how you feel. But Jessie was right. The Genritt boys are headin' for home. If we take the shortcut, we can be waitin' for them when they get there."

The proposal was sound. The brothers would be on the lookout the whole way back and might shoot the Ovaro out of spite if they were jumped. "How many more in the family?" Fargo asked.

"Four. Their ma, who is confined to a chair. Their pa, who is drunk half the time. And two brothers, who are just as mean as Buck and Morco."

"Lead the way."

Desma angled to the southeast, picking her way through the thick growth with astounding ease. Her bare feet made no sound on the soft soil. She constantly stepped on rocks and sticks, yet she never flinched.

Fargo found it difficult to concentrate with her so close. Her body was so supple, her legs so long and willowy, she stirred a hunger in him that had nothing to do with food. Her hair gave off a musty scent, a perfume she must have concocted herself, since it was unlikely she had the money to afford any. It tingled Fargo's nose and set him to thinking about how it would feel to run his hands through her lustrous mane.

The woodland gave way to open swamp. Desma advanced with care. Often strips of solid ground linked hummocks and islands, but just as often they had to wade through stagnant water that rose as high as their chests, surrounded by reeds and lilies that might harbor snakes or gators. It grated on a person's nerves.

Fargo saw two cottonmouths that swam off at their approach. Several alligators regarded them with dull interest but did not attack. Then they neared a small knob of land covered by high grass and stunted trees.

Desma was climbing out and reached for a limb for support. She was staring at the top of the knob or she would have seen bubbles froth under her arm and the large dark object that rose up out of the depths.

Fargo thought it was an alligator until the creature's triangular head and shell appeared and its hooked jaws opened wide to chomp down on the woman's arm. "Look out!" he shouted, grabbing her around the waist and heaving them both to the right just as the snapping turtle bit. It missed her by a hair.

They scrambled up out of the water, Fargo ready to shoot the thing if it came after them. Snapping turtles were slow but formidable. Once their jaws locked shut, it was next to impossible to pry them open. This one had to be over a yard long and weighed upward of two hundred pounds.

"It's an alligator snapper," Desma said breathlessly. "I would have lost my hand if it got hold of me." She exhaled, then lightly stroked his cheek. "I can't thank you enough for savin' me."

The snapper returned to its element in another display of bubbles. Fargo helped Desma to her feet, the warmth of her hand on his enough to make his groin twitch. A lump formed in his throat, and he coughed to clear it. "Don't you ever worry about what can happen to you out here?"

Desma shrugged. "Why fret over what might be? Life is for livin', Mr. Fargo. Not for worryin'."

On the other side was a long expanse of murky water. Fargo did not relish the thought of wading several hundred yards, so he was more than pleased to discover that they did not have to. Desma bore to the right to where an old log had been pulled up onto the knob.

"Give me a hand, will you?"

The log was not heavy. Over six feet long with a short length of limb jutting from the middle, it was child's play for the two of them to slide it in. Without ceremony Desma straddled it, hiking her dress partway up her thighs so it would not get more wet than it already was.

"We paddle with our hands," she said, and leaned low to demonstrate.

Fargo stroked smoothly, timing his to match hers. The log sailed along at a brisk clip, barreling through lilies, plowing through weeds. He tried to focus on the tract ahead, but the sheer beauty of Desma's thighs were enough to distract a monk. He could not stop admiring them. He could not stop thinking how nice it would be to have them wrapped around his waist.

To pass the time, Fargo said. "Tell me more about the Cajun. Connie mentioned that he was interested in you."

"All men are," Desma answered without looking back. "It is the price I pay for being female." She swatted at a bee that came too close. "As for Henri, there is not much to tell. He claims that he wants me, but I do not want him. I am not like Jasmine."

"Do you know where he lives?"

"No one does. He is a man of mystery, that one. There are those who say he has a place in Baton Rouge, others who claim he hails from New Orleans. He will be gone for many weeks at a time, then suddenly show up and lavish attention on a girl who more often than not will soon afterward vanish." Desma's tone turned flinty. "I tried to warn Jasmine. Everyone did. But she kept sayin' that no one had any proof he was bad. She let her heart rule her head, and it cost her dearly."

"What do you think happened to her and the others?"

"I wish I knew. If I were a man, I would beat the truth out of Lacombe."

That reminded Fargo. "Why haven't any of the local men done just that?"

"Most are afraid to go up against him and his men." Desma frowned. "You cannot blame them. They have families of their own to watch over." A water snake appeared directly ahead, a small fish in its mouth, and promptly plunged underwater to evade the log. "That brings up another way in which Lacombe is clever. The women who have disappeared have all been from families where there is no father, or where the father is known to be a weakling. He picks his victims well."

The disclosures gave Fargo a lot to think about. There had to be more to Lacombe's operation than simple abduction and murder. It had all the earmarks of a setup worthy of a big-city criminal ring, and that meant someone, somewhere, was getting rich off the scheme. Whatever it involved.

"I have sometimes wished I had been born a man," Desma took him unawares by saying. "I would not have put up with half the things I have."

"I'm glad you weren't," Fargo said. For his compliment he received an impish grin and a hint in her expression of something more.

Presently the log bumped to a stop at the base of a sizable island. Desma pulled it into a patch of bushes. "In case someone comes along. They would think it strange that a wet log was on dry ground." She smoothed her dress, covering those velvet thighs. "We're close, Skye. Very close."

A shallow marsh separated the island from a low ridge that in turn took them into a series of hills. Fargo was glad to be on firm footing again.

High up on a forested slope a column of smoke drifted. "That would be from the Genritt still," Desma said. "Before they came here they lived in Tennessee. I never saw folks so partial to corn whiskey in all my born days."

Fargo padded behind her to a trail that wound off up the hill in one direction and off into the swamp in another.

"That's the direction Buck and Morco will come from," Desma said, pointing. "I reckon it'll be pretty near an hour yet before they show. It's slow going with a horse." She flitted up the hill, as soundless as a moth taking wing.

They had not gone far when the sound of someone chopping wood fell on their ears. The *thunk-thunk-thunk* of a heavy ax guided them to a meadow where two brawny men were trimming a dead tree they had brought down.

"That's Lester Genritt," Desma said, indicating a man who had no forehead to speak of but more muscles than most five men combined. "He's the strongest of the brood. At a social once, he took a prize by lifting a grown bull clear off its feet."

Fargo made a mental note not to tangle with Lester.

"The other one is Silly Boy. His real name is Luke, but folks call him Silly Boy on account of all the pranks he's always playing." Desma snickered. "At that same social, he went and stuck the tail of a cat under the rockin' chair old Miss Wexler was rockin' in. That critter let out with a screech like a three-toed skunk ape's, and Miss Wexler came out of that chair as if her behind was on fire. It was downright comical."

Fargo doubted that Miss Wexler felt the same, but he made no comment. Screened by a thicket, he watched the brothers go about their business until Desma tapped him on the elbow.

"Follow me."

Their next stop was a stand of saplings that bordered a shelf midway up the hill. Here sat the clan's cabin, a structure that looked as if it had been strung together with bailing string and spit. A stiff wind would blow it right over, Fargo mused. He saw an elderly woman in a chair out front. Beside her rested three big hounds with wrinkled snouts and floppy ears, the kind favored by Southern backwoodsmen. They were big brutes, able to hold their own against bears and mountain lions.

"That's the ma," Desma stated the obvious. "Fletch, the father, must be up at the still. My ma swears that he spends his days lyin' under the tap with his mouth wide open."

"Let's get back down and find a spot to spring a surprise on Buck and Morco," Fargo said. Backing out of the saplings, he turned to go, and froze.

Twelve feet away stood a fourth hound, an enormous gray dog that bared its teeth and growled.

4

Skye Fargo inched his right hand toward his Colt as the stocky hound slunk toward him. He was confident that he could get off a shot before the dog tore into him, but he would rather not shoot if he could help it. The blast was bound to bring some of the Genritts on the run. The hound coiled its hind legs, preparing to charge. Gripping the butt of his revolver, he tensed for the rush.

It never came. Desma Collinder sashayed past him, chuckling softly and saying, "Why, Puddin', is that you? What are you doing out here by your lonesome? You should be sunnin' yourself with your brothers and your sister on the porch."

The gray hound relaxed. Whining like a puppy eager for affection, it nuzzled Desma when she squatted to rub its neck and scratch behind its ears. "Puddin' and me are old friends," she said quietly. "Fletch never goes anywhere without his dogs. He brings them to all the socials." She beckoned. "Here. Let him smell you so he'll know you from now on."

The dog's nose was cold to the touch. It sniffed, then licked Fargo's hand, caking his fingers with thick saliva.

"See? He's just a sweetheart once you get acquainted." Desma patted its head, motioned for the hound to go its own way, and moved on into the trees.

Fargo wiped his hand on the grass and followed her. They had gone a short distance when he looked back and discovered the dog was trailing them. He figured that it would soon lose interest and leave, but it did not. When they neared the meadow, where Lester and Silly Boy were working, he stopped. The dog might bark or do something else that would give them away, and he wanted Desma to get rid of it. He whispered her name.

She understood right away. Grinning, she hurried to Pudding and gave the animal a hug. "You must want some attention, big fella. But I just don't have the time to play right now. Run along." She gestured up the hill. "Shoo, Puddin'! Go on, now!"

The hound looked at her with its great sad eyes and did not budge.

"Scat!" Desma said more forcefully. "Run along and chase rabbits or something." Picking up a stick, she hurled it as far as she could. "Fetch, boy! Go get it!"

Fargo was watching their antics. He did not hear any footsteps. He had no warning that anyone else was within hundreds of feet of them until someone behind him snorted.

"You're wastin' your time, gorgeous. That idiot never was much good at tricks. If it's sticks you want fetched, you should play with Hominy. She'll chase 'em for hours."

Lester and Silly Boy Genritt were side by side, Silly Boy holding a shotgun leveled at Fargo. He wore a crooked grin, and his right eyelid kept twitching. "Howdy, stranger. Mind tellin' us what you're doing here?"

"He's with me," Desma came to Fargo's defense, moving over to stand next to him. "I'm showin' him around. We were passin' by when Puddin' latched onto us."

Silly Boy blatantly ogled her lush form. "Strange. You've never come out this way any other time. How come you seen fit to do it now with this stranger?"

Desma adopted a charming smile. "What's the matter, Silly Boy? Don't tell me that you're jealous?"

"No," Silly Boy declared, but his blush put the lie to his statement.

"Why, I never knew you cared," Desma teased, waltzing

over to him and touching him on the tip of his stubbly chin. He turned even darker and lowered the shotgun.

"Shucks. I reckon you can come by our place anytime you get a notion to. But you'd better run along before Pa catches you. He doesn't cotton to strangers much."

"Thank you," Desma said sweetly. Winking at Fargo, she started to go past the brothers when the huge brooding specimen seized her by the arm.

"No. You're comin' with us, girl. You and your fancy friend."

Desma twisted, trying to pry loose. "Whatever for? What's gotten into you, Lester Genritt? Unhand me this instant."

Lester shook his head. "Pa gave orders that no strangers are to be on our property without his say-so. We're to bring anyone we catch to him and Ma."

"But, Lester, it's *me*," Desma said. "We've known each other for years. Let me go and we'll be on our way."

"No."

Desma glanced at Silly Boy, pleading with her eyes. Silly Boy scowled at his bigger brother and made as if to interfere, but then he thought better of the idea and jerked his shotgun up to cover Fargo. "I'm sorry, gorgeous. Les is right. Pa did give us orders. I'll get my backside blistered if I don't do as he wants."

Fargo was itching to go for his Colt. It would not be long before Morco and Buck got there. But the unwavering barrel of the shotgun rooted him in place. At that range, it would about blow him in half. His only hope was that Desma could distract Silly Boy somehow.

Lester suddenly shook her. "Quit, squirmin', girl. I don't want to hurt you, but you have to behave or I just might." He started forward. "Now, let's go see what Pa and Ma have to say about all this."

The gray hound, belly low to the ground, moved in front of the hulking backwoodsman and rumbled deep in its broad chest.

"What the hell?" Lester said. "Get out of my way, you dumb dog, or else."

Pudding growled again, managing to look savage despite all the wrinkles. Slinking closer, the hound bared its teeth as it had earlier.

Silly Boy found the whole thing amusing. "Stupid dog!" he said, laughing. "He always did have a soft spot for a pretty face. Remember that time he followed the Honicker sisters home from the church picnic?"

Lester did not stop. Maybe he believed that the hound would not attack one of its own masters. Maybe he thought that it would give way because it would not dare to go up against someone his size. Or maybe he figured that the kick he aimed at its head would drive it off. On all counts he was wrong. For as he kicked, the dog launched itself at him, clamped its jaws onto his free arm, and held on.

A howl of pain burst from Lester's lips. Releasing Desma, he grabbed the hound by the scruff of its neck and yanked, striving to pull it off.

"I'll be damned!" Silly Boy blurted. Forgetting about Fargo, he went to the assistance of his brother but had to leap back when Lester commenced swinging the dog from side to side as if it were a sack of grain.

It was the moment Fargo had been waiting for. Intending to knock Silly Boy out, he drew the Colt. Silly Boy saw him, though, and spun, bringing the shotgun up one more time. Fargo banged off a shot before the Tennessean could, his slug tearing into Silly Boy's shoulder and slamming the notorious prankster flat. In reflex Silly Boy jerked on the trigger, and the shotgun discharged into the ground.

The next moment a lumbering mountain smashed into Fargo. "You shot Luke!" Lester railed, clubbing Fargo with fists the size of hams. Fargo fell to his knees, aware of blood splattering his face from the wound in Lester's left wrist. A few yards away Pudding lay, stunned.

"I'll squash you like a bug!" Lester fumed. Encircling

Fargo with his python arms, Lester hoisted him into the air and applied more pressure. "First I'm going to break every bone in your stinkin' body, then I'm going to stomp you to a pulp!"

Fargo had no breath to respond. It felt as if his chest were caught in a vise. His arms trapped at his sides, he fought to break the hulk's grip. But he was like a child in the grasp of a giant, his strength no match for Genritt's sinews. His wits had to compensate for the backwoodsman's brawn.

Lester leered as he constricted his arms even farther. "Gettin' hard to breath yet, mister?" he gloated. "Soon you'll hear your own ribs crack and pop, and that will just be the beginnin'."

Think so? Fargo wanted to say. Instead, he rammed his knee into the bigger man's groin, not once but three times, and after the third blow Lester grunted and sagged a few inches, his grip slackening. Fargo's feet touched the ground. Digging in his heels for leverage, he pushed off, propelling Lester backward toward the prone hound. His ruse worked. Lester tripped over Pudding and went down, letting go as he fell.

Fargo was to his knees ahead of the backwoodsman. He slammed the Colt's barrel against Lester's brow. It rocked Lester, but he continued to straighten so Fargo slugged him again, putting everything he had into a blow to the temple that caused Lester to keel to the right like a listing ship. Still, Lester did not go down, though. Fargo pounded him again. It did the trick.

Desma rushed toward him. Fargo assumed she was concerned for his welfare and said, "I'm all right, thanks." But she never gave him a glance. Kneeling beside Pudding, she ran a hand over the dog's head and neck. It lifted itself high enough to lick her, then rolled onto its stomach, slowly but surely recovering.

"Thank God!" Desma said. "For a minute there I feared that brute had broken its neck."

Fargo had more important considerations than the hound. The father and mother could not help but hear the gunshots, which meant the father and the rest of the hounds were bound to show up soon. Grabbing Desma's hand, he sped down the trail toward the swamp. They passed the meadow, slanting to the left when the trail did.

Below, where the trail came up out of the swamp, figures appeared. Fargo darted up onto a mound choked by high weeds and hunkered. "Damn," he fumed.

Buck and Morco had arrived. They had heard the shots and had their guns cocked as they hastened up the slope, Buck in the lead, pulling on the Ovaro's reins.

"What will you do?" Desma whispered in Fargo's ear. "They know something is wrong. They'll be harder to take now."

Fargo agreed. And as if that were not bad enough, from up the hill wavered the deep-throated bay of hounds unleashed. It would take a minute or so for the dogs to find where Lester and Silly Boy lay, perhaps another thirty to forty seconds for them to pick up the scent and keep on coming. That gave Fargo less than two minutes to do what had to be done.

Buck and Morco were moving as quickly as they could. They were fifteen feet below the mound when Buck thrust the reins at his younger brother and said, "You hold onto these. I'm going on ahead to see what's happened."

"Why should you go?" Morco objected. "I can run a heap faster than you do."

"Just do as I say, dammit!" Buck snarled. Flinging the reins, he sped up the hill. His brother stomped a foot in annoyance, cursed a few times, then turned to the stallion and raised the Remington as if to take out his frustration on the pinto.

That Fargo would not allow. He rose to his feet, the Colt

at his side. "Hello, horse thieves," he greeted them. Both glanced up in shock. Buck was the first to recover, the first to bring his weapon into play, sweeping the Sharps to his shoulder to snap off a round. Fargo fanned a single shot that cored Buck's head, sending him in a tumble down the trail. Morco had the Remington extended and fired, but his shot was hasty. Fargo's was not.

Leaping from the mound, Fargo raced to the stallion. It stood as docile as a lamb as he scooped up the reins and gave it a hasty inspection. Mud caked its legs from its hooves to its chest, with additional splotches dotting its hide from its shoulder to its flank. Otherwise it was none the worse for wear. The Henry rested in the saddle scabbard, where it should be. His other effects had not been touched.

"What are you waitin' for?" Desma prompted.

The baying of the oncoming hounds emphasized the urgency. Fargo holstered the Colt and forked leather, swinging her on behind him. She glued her full form to his, her slender arms looped around his waist, her hands inches above his manhood. It seemed a wholly unconscious act on her part, and Fargo did not think much of it.

Spurring the Ovaro around, he trotted into the swamp, using the trail the Genritt brothers had. The baying of the hounds took on a new note. A glance showed them milling around Buck's body. A big black grave voice to a raspy bellow, and the three dogs bounded on down the slope to Morco. There they barely paused. A brown and yellow dog caught sight of the Ovaro, tilted its head to the heavens, and voiced a high-pitched cry. It was the signal for the trio to bolt in pursuit.

Fargo was at a disadvantage. He did not know the terrain, and the danger of blundering into quicksand or deep water that might harbor snakes and gators made him hold the stallion to a brisk walk.

The hounds rapidly gained. Fargo yanked the Henry from the scabbard. As reluctant as he was to slay the dogs, he would not let them get close enough to do the stallion or the woman any harm.

"No, wait!" Desma said. Without warning she hopped off and turned.

Hauling on the reins, Fargo brought the Ovaro broadside to the trail. He sighted on the lead hound, ready to shoot if it did not stop before it came within springing range.

Desma held her hands aloft and beamed at them as if they were long-lost friends. "Hominy! Lazarus! Andrew Jackson! Stop right there!"

If it were possible for hounds to look confused, these certainly did. They slowed, the big brown and yellow one whining and wagging its tail.

"You know me," Desma went on in a silken, soothing tone. "We're old friends. Remember that time I fed all of you some leftover catfish?" As she talked, she walked slowly toward them, swaying as if in time to music only she could hear. The effect on the dogs was as hypnotic as it had been on Pudding. They halted, all three whining now, eager to please her. Laughing gaily, she knelt and embraced each one in turn. Petting them and whispering into their ears, she soon had them acting like puppies.

"See?" Desma said, smirking. "Dogs are just like men. All a woman has to do is smile and bat her eyelashes, and she can wrap them around her little finger."

Fargo stared up the hill. The father would be along soon. Lester and Silly Boy might be with him if they had revived. "Let's light a shuck for the Tanner cabin," he advised.

Desma gave each of the hounds a farewell pat, then let herself be levered up onto the back of the stallion. She blew kisses to the dogs as they sat and watched her depart. "The poor dears. They look just like Henri Lacombe did when I told him that I would not go out with him if he were the last man on earth."

Fargo knuckled down to negotiating the swamp without mishap. It was growing late, and he wondered if they would reach the Tanner homestead before dark. Mentioning it, he added, "What about your mother? Won't she be upset if you're not home before sunset?"

"I'm a big girl and can do as I please. She doesn't care one way or the other."

Fargo remembered the Kentucky rifle shoved in his face. "You could have fooled me."

Desma guessed what he was referring to. "She thought you were one of Lacombe's men. She was doing what any mother would do, protectin' her child." Desma sobered. "If my pa were still alive, he would have taken that Cajun, strung him up by his feet over a nest of cottonmouths, then cut the rope a single strand at a time."

They pushed on, Fargo keeping track of the sun. It hung on the rim of the world when he emerged from the heavy timber that grew near the Tanner cabin.

Little Jessica was perched on the porch waiting for them. "Ma! Ma! They're here!" she squealed, dashing across the yard.

The moment Fargo dismounted, the girl threw herself into his arms. It caught him by surprise. He was not accustomed to being around children, and certainly not to having one he hardly knew act so affectionate. As Constance hurried outdoors, an apron over her dress, he set Jessica down and announced, "I can't stay long. I should take Desma home so her mother doesn't worry." No matter what Desma said, he wouldn't put it past her mother to take it out on him if she learned the two of them had been together and Desma did not get home at a proper hour.

"Nonsense," Connie said. "The two of you can stay the night. I'll explain everything to Virginia. She'll understand." Connie wiped her hands on the apron. "Besides, supper will be done in a short while, and I made extra in the hope you would join us. It's been a spell since we had a gentleman in the house."

"Oh, please stay!" Jessica begged.

Fargo's stomach growled at the mention of food. He had not eaten a meal all day. The lengthening shadows made up his mind for him. That, and the memory of how closely Desma had held him on their long ride through the bayous. "I guess I will," he said.

It turned out to be a wise choice.

The meal was delicious, a home-cooked bonanza that included fried chicken, potatoes, dumplings, several vegetables, soup, and cornbread. Fargo got the impression that Constance had outdone herself on his behalf, and he did justice to her effort by downing three helpings and polishing it off with five cups of coffee. He was filled near to bursting when he pushed his plate back and went out onto the porch for some fresh air. Desma was already there. Jessica started to follow him but had to go back in when her mother called.

"They're nice folks," Fargo commented.

"The best. It's a pity about Jasmine." Desma was leaning against a post, her profile caught in silhouette by the rising full moon. She had a sensuous glow about her that had nothing to do with the moonlight.

The talk during supper had mainly revolved around Henri Lacombe and the missing women. But Fargo had learned a few personal facts as well. Such as how Constance had been scrimping and saving so that one day she could send her daughters to a fine school for girls in New Orleans "so they can make something of themselves." He also learned that it was Desma who had taught Jessica how to read and write. The raven-tressed lovely tutored half a dozen children, each once a week in marathon three-hour sessions. It was the only schooling the children were likely to receive. Most would grow up to live as their parents, eking out a living as best they could from the hostile land. Only the strongest survived in bayou country. The rest were swallowed up as neatly as a snapper would swallow a fish.

"Care to go for a stroll?" Desma asked.

Fargo agreed, hoping she had in mind the same thing he did. But she walked to one side, her hands behind her back, the pale light bathing her lovely features, giving her the aspect of animated marble. She was breathtaking.

"Do you have any idea where to begin your search?" Desma wanted to know.

"I have a hunch there is someone in Possum Hollow who can help me out," Fargo said, and did not elaborate. The breeze brought the chirp of crickets, the croak of frogs, the deeper bellow of alligators seeking to attract mates. He knew how they felt.

"Be watchin' your back every step of the way," Desma cautioned. "The cutthroats you're up against have no scruples. They'd as soon stick a dagger between your shoulder blades as look at you."

"I haven't lasted this long by being careless," Fargo responded. She was leading him in the general direction of the pool claimed by Old Broken Tooth, and he heard the old gator join in the chorus of its fellows. A few yards farther and she skipped off to the right, passing behind him toward a knoll that rose to the northwest.

"Last one to the top is a rotten egg."

It was a child's game, but Fargo joined in. Her carefree attitude was contagious. He relished her laughter as she bounded up the steep grade with all the speed and grace of an antelope. It took all he had to beat her, and at that he only won by a few yards. Grinning, she congratulated him, then stepped to the edge overlooking the swamp to catch her breath. He swore he could feel the heat her body gave off as she glided by.

Desma reminded Fargo of a thoroughbred in its prime. She was young, filled with zest, pulsing with life and vigor. One day a man would come along who would strike her fancy, and they would plant roots somewhere and raise darling little sprouts like Jessica. Fargo found himself envying her husband, whoever it would be. The lucky gent was in for a ride through life that most men would trade anything for.

But Fargo was not one of them. As much as he liked her, marriage was just not in the cards for him. His wanderlust always kept him on the go, roaming where few had roamed before, seeing all there was to see.

Desma's dusky scent filled his nostrils. She materialized in front of him, her warm breath on his cheek, her eyes drilling into him as if she were trying to peer into the depths of his soul. "Most men would have been pawin' all over me by now. Why haven't you done anything?"

"There are times when it's best to let the woman make the first move. That way there are no hard feelings if the man is overstepping his boundary."

"Think you know it all, don't you?" Desma said, smirking. She leaned closer, her ripe lips nearly brushing his. "If it's a clue you want, maybe this will do."

With that, she kissed him.

5

It was more than just any kiss. It was sugary sweet and wonderfully warm, her lips as tasty as fresh cherries, as soft as a feather pillow. Desma pressed her body against his, the two of them joining as if they were two halves of a hole. Her breasts mashed against his chest, her thighs ground into his. The heat she gave off now was caused by more than exertion. She was an inferno, a cauldron on the verge of bubbling over.

Fargo's manhood surged, straining for release. He slid his tongue into her mouth, and hers danced around his, enticing, tempting, teasing. His right hand roved down Desma's back, his left slid between them to flatten against her smooth stomach. From there it drifted upward to cup her left breast.

From the depths of Desma's throat came a fluttering groan. She sucked on his tongue as if it were hard candy. Her fingernails dug into his shoulders. Her left leg entwined around his.

The top of the knoll was an oval grassy bed. Fargo gently lowered her down in the center and stretched out beside her. The moonlight washing over Desma's upturned face lent her features an angelic aspect, as if she were more than mere flesh and blood. That she was both Fargo proved by cupping her right breast and eliciting a hungry moan.

Desma hooked an arm around his neck to pull him closer, her tongue finding his. Her other hand massaged his chest and slowly worked lower. There was no shy streak in her, no sham modesty. She knew what she wanted, and she threw herself into their coupling with the same zest she always exhibited.

Fargo's own hunger mounted. He got the top of her dress undone and slipped his hand inside, his palm settling on a hard nipple that grew even harder. Exposing her breast, he abruptly bent and closed his mouth over it. He tweaked the nipple, lathered her globe, while she panted and locked her fingers in his hair. His hat fell off.

"I knew you would be good," Desma husked.

Fargo was glad that he was not disappointing her. He freed her other breast and switched back and forth, stimulating both until they were as full as ripe melons. He had lost track of her roaming hand and suddenly felt it close on his organ. She stroked him lightly, the sensation too exquisite for words.

At the back of his mind, though, a tiny voice railed that he was letting his lust get the better of him. They were out in the open, close to a swamp choked with snakes and gators. At any moment something might come crawling by. Or, worse, little Jessica would show up, and they would give her the shock of her young life.

All such worries were dashed when Desma slid her hand inside his pants to cup the stem of his pole. At that moment Fargo would not have cared if Old Broken Tooth walked up and bit him on the hind end. He glued his mouth to hers, giving her a kiss that literally took her breath away.

Desma cooed like a dove in love, wriggling her bottom in anticipation. She licked his jaw, his neck, his ear, her lips closing on his lobe, her breath warm and tingly. The whole time her hand inside his pants was busy stoking his coals, raising his temperature to match her own. She knew just what to do, too, never handling him roughly, never squeezing too hard.

Fargo had no idea if her skill stemmed from experience or just a natural knack. Nor did he really care. He was immersed in their lovemaking, submerging himself in the pool of her desire. Sensations ruled them both, sensations of raw pleasure. They were living for the moment, and that moment was the mutual fulfillment of their fiery passion.

Desma tugged at his belt, unhitching it, then loosened his pants. Both of her hands wrapped around his member and began a rhythmic up and down motion that made Fargo arch his back. He bit his lower lip, fighting for self-control, hating to spoil everything by exploding too soon. She seemed to sense his dilemma and brought one of her hands up to his shoulders.

"Nice and easy, handsome. That's how I like it."

So did Fargo. He devoted himself to her mounds, to her stomach, to the smooth-as-glass swell of her inner thighs. She kissed, she licked, she even bit, her hips bucking with mounting urgency. One of her hands raked his back, his buttocks. Moans without cease fluttered on the night breeze.

Fargo hiked her dress up to her waist. She parted her legs to grant him access, sighing loudly when his probing fingers found her damp slit. He inserted his middle one, and it was her turn to arch her spine, her mouth agape, her eyes wide with carnal craving. The musty scent that engulfed them was more tantalizing than the most expensive perfume.

"Oooooohhhhhhhhh," Desma said.

Stroking her, Fargo lowered his pants down to his knees. Her inner walls closed around his finger, adding to the friction, preparing her for what was to come next. He took his sweet time. It was ten minutes before he replaced his finger with his pole, doing it so adroitly that he was inside her to the hilt before she realized what he had done. When she did, her legs locked around his hips and she kissed him as if it were the last kiss either of them would ever know.

"Do it. Do it, please."

Fargo wanted to oblige her, but he held off for both their sakes, prolonging the inevitable as long as his body could endure the strain. Pacing himself, he rocked back and forth on his knees, rocking, rocking, rocking until Desma gasped, clasped him tight, and heaved against him as if attempting to break him in half. He knew the signs, so he met her thrusts with matching slams of his whole body, driving into her like a human sledgehammer. She called out his name and other words no one could understand, inarticulate cries that signified she had crested and was lost in the most wonderful delirium known to humankind.

It was not long before Fargo followed suit. The blast ripped him from the base of his spine to the crown of his head. His toes curled, his breath caught in his throat. The stars spun, the lights of the cabin swirled, the night sounds blended into his outcry and hers, and for an instant he had the illusion that everything there was had been caught up in the fervor of their rapture.

Then the moment passed. The illusion faded. Fargo coasted down to earth, sagging on top of Desma. She was breathing heavily, her skin caked with sweat. Contentment sparkled in her eyes.

"You were magnificent."

"I aim to please," Fargo joked, rolling off so she could breathe easier. Her fingers crept into his hair. She pecked him on the cheek, then snuggled against him for warmth. Now that they had stopped, the cool breeze chilled them both. But neither was in any rush to dress and go.

"Skye?" Desma said.

Fargo tensed. It was at such awkward moments that most women wanted to know if he had ever thought about having a wife and a home. "What?"

"I want to thank you for coming all this way to help out Jessie. She was heartbroken when Jasmine vanished."

Fargo said nothing. They were both aware that he was bucking the odds trying to find the older sister. She might be anywhere. In New Orleans. In another state. Or dead.

"You must be wonderin' where Jessie got the notion to

write to you," Desma went on dreamily. "Well, one day when I was schooling her, I had her read from a newspaper. It was a few months old, but it told about the sharpshootin' contest you were in over to Springfield, Missouri. Do you remember it?"

How could he forget? Fargo reflected. Four of the finest sharpshooters alive had been invited to compete, and the promoter had made sure that every paper carried the story.

"The newspaper mentioned how you're one of the best trackers around, and how you've scouted and hunted pretty near from one end of the country to the other. Jessie got all excited readin' it. She said that if anyone could find Jasmine, it would be you." Desma smiled. "The poor dear begged me to help her write you. How was I to say no?"

"You did the right thing."

"I hope so," Desma said. "Because it will break her heart all over again if you don't bring Jasmine back alive and well. Jessie sees you as the answer to her prayers. Every night before bedtime she prayed that you would come."

"I hope I don't disappoint her," Fargo responded. Which was an understatement. The last thing he wanted to do was shatter the child's hopes. Some girls Jessie's age were as fragile as china. If they were broken too many times, they could never be mended.

The wind grew stronger. Fargo took that as a cue to get dressed. Desma clasped his hand as they walked down the knoll, a bounce in her step that had not been there before. Mother and daughter were waiting for them on the porch, Connie rocking and knitting, Jessie playing with dominoes.

"There you are!" the child declared. "Where have you been? I was gettin' worried, but Ma wouldn't let me go look for you."

Desma patted the girl's head. "You had no cause to fret yourself. We were takin' a walk, is all."

"Did you hear that strange critter?" Jessie asked, rising. Her mother began to knit faster.

"Critter?" Desma said.

Jessie pointed toward the knoll. "We heard it a couple of times. It made a sound sort of like a bird, but it wasn't no bird. Once I heart a grunt, like a big old bear was out there. I asked Ma to take the rifle and go see, but she said we were better off close to the house."

Fargo went inside for his bedroll and the Henry. Constance had offered him a bed, but there were only two and he was averse to putting anyone out on his account. As he stepped out again, Jessie snatched hold of his arm.

"You're not fixin' to turn in already, are you, Mr. Fargo? I was hopin' we could sit up and talk awhile."

"Sorry" Fargo said. "I need to get an early start, and it's been a long day." She reluctantly let go, and he headed for the side of the cabin.

"You're makin' a mistake," Jessie said in parting. "Whatever is out there might decide to eat you. What would you do then?"

"Ask it to chew quietly so it doesn't wake me up." Fargo nodded at the laughing women and went around the corner. The Ovaro was tied out back. He spread out his blanket near the rear wall, used his saddle as a pillow, and laid down with the Henry at his side. He would have preferred that it be Desma, but he contented himself with recalling how soft and supple her skin had been as he drifted into dreamland.

True to his word, Fargo was mounted by first light. He walked the stallion to the front of the cabin to avoid waking the others. To his surprise, all three were up and on the porch, Desma and Connie wrapped in shawls, Jessie in a robe that must have been her mother's when her mother was about the same age.

"We thought it proper to see you off," Constance said. She brought him a small bundle wrapped in buckskin. "Jerky and such for when you're hungry."

Desma did not say a word. Her eyes misting, she waved

at him as he trotted toward the trail that would eventually take him to Possum Hollow.

Jessie waved and yelled and bounced up and down, making enough noise to rouse every alligator within five miles. Her parting words were, "Bring Jasmine back to us in one piece!"

The day dawned crisp and clear. It was not until the middle of the morning that the oppressive heat and humidity combined to make an oven of the swamp. Fargo had learned his lesson on his trek out and did not go anywhere near any of the homesteads he passed. Twice he saw backwoodsmen who blended into the vegetation when they spotted him.

Possum Hollow was the same. The same chickens were roaming in the same dusty rutted track, the same hog was in noisy evidence, the same dogs were lounging in the shade. Fargo circled around behind the general store, cradled the Henry, and entered through the back door. Apparently Big Bob lived there as well as worked there, judging by a filthy kitchen Fargo crossed that had a cot in the corner.

A dark hall led past a supply room to the store proper. It was empty save for Big Bob, who sat at a table playing solitaire, his back to the hall.

Fargo cat-footed forward, setting each boot down carefully so his spurs would not jangle. He was right behind the proprietor when the man must have sensed another presence and shifted to glance over a bulky shoulder. Fargo hit him. He smashed the rifle's stock against Big Bob's temple, and the man crashed to the floor, chair and all, almost upsetting the table as well.

Dumbfounded, Big Bob sat there with a flabby hand over the welt, gawking in disbelief.

"I'm only going to ask this once," Fargo said. "Where is Jasmine Tanner?"

Fury made Big Bob quake. "How the hell should I know? What gives you the right to walk into a man's store and beat him over the head? You're lucky you caught me by surprise or—"

Fargo hit him again, a blow to the other temple.

The massive man sagged but did not fall flat, a trickle of blood where the flesh had split. His pudgy jowls quivered anew as he propped a hand under him and tried to rise. "Damn your hide!" he roared. "I'll have you strung up for this! See if I don't!"

Waiting until Big Bob was on one knee, Fargo hit him once more. This time he drove the barrel into the man's ribs so hard that Bob yelped and fell onto his side. Holding the spot, Big Bob grimaced, then pounded the floor. "You stinking saddle tramp! Don't do that again or you'll be sorry! I have friends hereabouts who will carve your guts up—"

A boot in the stomach sufficed to shut Big Bob up. Fargo loomed over him, the Henry upraised. "Jasmine Tanner," he said.

Fear flared in the proprietor's dark eyes. Holding a hand out to ward off the blow, he replied, "What makes you think that I know where she is? I'm not her kin. She could be anywhere, for cryin' out loud."

Fargo was tired of being lied to. Slamming the stock into the crown of Big Bob's head, he stepped aside as Bob folded and lay prone, out to the world. Fargo walked behind the counter, selected a whiskey bottle, then took a seat in the same chair Big Bob had sat in. After enjoying a long swig, he took a red ten that Big Bob had placed on a red jack and switched it to a black jack. He played for a while, the only sounds the oinking of the hog out front and the deep breathing of the human one next to the table.

At last Bob groaned. His eyelids fluttered. He rolled onto his back and began to rise, freezing when he set eyes on Fargo. "I was hopin you'd left," he said sullenly.

Fargo deposited the cards and filled his hand with the

Colt. The other man's mouth twitched as he made a show of thumbing back the hammer and pointing the pistol.

"You wouldn't!" Big Bob blurted.

In response, Fargo sent a slug into the floor between Bob's legs, so close to Bob's crotch that Bob yelped and tried to scoot backward on his posterior. Fargo curled back the hammer again, the click quite distinct. "You're wasting my time," he warned. "We both know that you have the information I need."

Bob was still defiant. "You're not right in the head, mister. You don't have any proof that I'm involved with what happened to her or any of those other girls."

Fargo exercised patience. He had time on his side. "You lied to me about the Tanner family, remember? And the only reason you did was because you didn't want me finding them. You suspected that I was here about Jasmine."

"That's not proof. It's just your opinion."

Ignoring him, Fargo took another swig. "It wasn't hard for me to figure out that you have to be helping Lacombe find his victims once I learned what was going on."

The accusation flustered Big Bob. "That Cajun and me? Be serious. It would be suicide. The way some folks feel about him, they would string me up if they thought there was any link between the two of us."

"That they would," Fargo agreed. "So maybe I should call everyone together and point out that Lacombe is a newcomer here, that he has to have someone working for him who knows the people in the area. Someone who tells him which young women are the prettiest, which ones don't have fathers or big brothers to look out for them."

"It ain't me!" Big Bob said.

Motioning at the merchandise on the shelves, Fargo said, "Your general store is the only one between here and Baton Rouge. Homesteaders come to you from miles around. You probably know each and every one by their first names."

He pointed the Colt at the proprietor's groin. "It can't be anyone else. So how much is Lacombe paying you?"

"It could be anyone. Not just me," Big Bob said. But his voice, his eyes, his posture, they all told otherwise. "Please. You have to believe me."

"I don't," Fargo said, then shot him in the fleshy part of the thigh.

Screeching hysterically, Bob flopped about like a fish out of water, his fingers spread over the wound to stem the bleeding. When the hammer ratcheted back yet again, he held himself perfectly still and looked up, petrified with fear. "All right! All right! He pays me forty dollars every time I come up with the name of a gal who turns out to be the kind he's interested in."

"What does he do with them?" Fargo probed.

"I don't know," Big Bob said, screaming it louder when Fargo sighted down the pistol. "Honest to God, I don't! He's real secretive about where he takes them."

Hiding his disappointment, Fargo said, "You must have overhead a remark or two. You must have some idea."

"If I did, I'd tell you," Big Bob stated. His fingers were caked with blood. He bent to see the wound better and whimpered. "The only thing I do know is that when the Cajun is around, he stays at an old shack about six miles northeast of here. It was abandoned by the folks who built it years ago."

"What part do the Genritts have in all this?" Fargo inquired.

"Those bumpkins? No part at all. The reason they went along with my lie about the Tanners was because they thought I was playing a trick on you," Bob added as an afterthought. "They hate strangers."

Fargo had a final question. But just then Big Bob glanced at the entrance, grinned slyly, and hollered, "Boys! Help me! This skunk is trying to steal my money!"

Fargo did not turn to learn who was behind him. He

threw himself from the chair, grabbing the Henry as he dived. A pair of rifles boomed the instant he did. Landing on his shoulder, he rolled behind a different chair and pushed to one knee with it between him and the doorway. Framed under the lintel were Lester and Silly Boy Genritt, Silly Boy with a bandaged shoulder. They hastily backed out as he snapped a shot that clipped the jamb.

Quiet reigned, broken by a peculiar bubbling sound from near the bar. The two slugs meant for Fargo had struck Big Bob, one in the chest, the other in the jaw. Half his mouth was gone. From it gushed crimson froth. From his chest pumped a steady scarlet stream. His wide eyes focused on Fargo, and he tried to say something. A hand lifted, opened, and thudded limply to the floor.

Fargo thought he heard footsteps. One of the brothers was circling around to the back of the building so they could cover both doors. Holstering the Colt, he picked up the chair in his left hand and moved to the wall next to the entrance. Coiling, he heaved the chair out into the sunlight.

A rifle cracked. A muffled curse gave Silly Boy's position away. He was somewhere to the right, probably at the corner of the store. Lester was the one watching the rear.

Working swiftly, Fargo lined up two more chairs close to the doorway. He threw the first and heard Silly Boy titter. The prankster was not about to fall for the same trick twice. Certainly not three times. But Fargo hurled the third chair anyway and listened to Silly Boy laugh. Silly Boy was still laughing when Fargo hurtled out the entrance just seconds after the last chair.

The youngest brother was caught flat-footed, his rifle slanted at the ground. He tried to bring it up, his laughter changing to a curse that died on his lips when the Henry thundered twice and a pair of .44-caliber slugs ripped through his chest.

Fargo rose, his back to the wall. From the back of the store Lester bellowed.

"Luke? Did you get him?"

Turning to the left, Fargo moved rapidly to where Big Bob's horse was tied. Possum Hollow was more deserted than ever. Even the chickens and the hogs had gone into hiding when the gunfire broke out. The horse pricked its ears but did not whinny as he moved to the rail and from there to the rear corner. A peek failed to reveal Lester.

Fargo went on. His hunch was that the hulking Genritt had gone around to the front to find out why Luke had not answered. He dashed into the back doorway, across the kitchen, retracing the steps he had taken just a short while ago, anxious to reach the front quickly. Sprinting down the hall, he gave no regard to the supply room. It never occurred to him that Lester might be inside.

Then something slammed into Fargo's back with such force that he was knocked flat. Nearly senseless, he groped for the Henry.

Fingers as thick as iron spikes closed on his neck. "You're going to die slowly, mister. One part of you at a time."

6

Skye Fargo was snapped up off the floor so violently that his upper and lower teeth cracked together. Agony jolted him out of his daze. He looked up just as Lester shoved him into a wall, barely getting an arm up to cushion some of the impact.

"That's it, mister. Fight me," Lester said. "I'll like it more that way."

Fargo pried at the fingers constricting his neck, but it was impossible to loosen them. He was swung to the right, then to the left, then raised bodily off the floor and flung like a potato sack. He did not know if he collided with a wall or the floor, but whatever it was left him lying on his left side, as weak as a lamb. A shadow stomped into sight, taking definite shape. Lester's twisted, bloodthirsty features leaned toward him.

"Come on, stranger. You can do better than this. Give me a tussle."

A calloused hand pumped Fargo into the air. He clawed at the Colt and started to draw it, but it was torn from his grasp. Lester cuffed him four times, each so hard that his ears rang. His tormentor chortled as he was unceremoniously dumped on the floor.

"No weapons, bastard. Just the two of us, man to man. I'd call that fair, wouldn't you?"

No one would call that fair. Lester outweighed Fargo by eighty or ninety pounds, every ounce muscle. It was like pitting a cougar against a grizzly. The cougar, while formidable in its own right, was vastly overmatched. Fargo's sole hope lie in unsheathing his lone fang. Accordingly, as he lay slumped over, he slid his right hand to his right boot. He had to hike his pant leg to get at the Arkansas toothpick.

"Let's see. What should I do next?" Lester said. Seizing Fargo by the shoulders, Lester shook him savagely, then hurled him down the hall.

Fargo slid to a crashing halt against the doorway into the main part of the store. He was on his stomach, his knees curled. Lying still to deceive the backwoodsman into thinking that he was too weak to resist any further, he again lifted his pant leg and this time closed his hand around the slim knife.

Lester's big feet tromped closer. "This ain't nearly as much fun as I thought it would be," he complained. "Can't you at least fight back a little bit?"

Fargo gauged the distance between them while tightening every sinew in his body. Marshaling all his might, he waited until Lester was almost on top of him. Then he unwound, sweeping erect, thrusting the toothpick out and up. The blade sliced into Lester's neck. It was Fargo's aim to sever his foe's jugular, but Genritt jerked to the left.

"*Damn you!*" Lester roared. He had spared his throat, but his neck bore an ugly gash darkened by spreading blood. Touching it gingerly, he glowered at the drops on his fingertips. "No more toyin' with you, mister. It's to the finish now."

Fargo would not have it any other way. He ducked under a fist that would have caved in his skull, retaliating with a slash of the toothpick that opened Lester's arm from the elbow to the wrist.

Back-pedaling, Lester gaped at the wound and the crimson color seeping into his shirtsleeve. "You hurt me again!" he declared, as if it were the most astonishing fact in the world. "No one has ever hurt me before."

Fargo moved forward. A wary look came into Lester's eyes, and he crouched, his huge hands held loosely in front of him, his weight resting on the balls of his feet. Despite his ponderous bulk, Lester was agile and quick. Fargo dared not underestimate him.

Lunging, Fargo nicked Lester's right hand. He tried to imbed the toothpick in Lester's chest, but Lester danced out of range, continuing to slowly retreat down the hall. Fargo assumed that Genritt was trying to reach the kitchen where he would have more room to maneuver. Lester, though, angled toward the wall. Fargo did not understand why until he saw the doorway to the supply room. Leaning against it was Lester's rifle.

Darting forward, Fargo unleashed a flurry designed to drive Lester away from the supply room. Lester did skip to the left. But as Fargo drew his arm back from another stab, the backwoodsman pounced, grabbing Fargo's wrist and holding on to prevent Fargo from wielding the toothpick. Lester's other hand streaked to Fargo's neck.

"Now it's my turn, puny man. I'm going to rip your throat out with my bare hands."

In a fight it was not wise to talk too much. Long ago Fargo had learned that when it came time to kill, kill and be done with it. Needless chatter could distract a man at the wrong moment. It was a lesson Lester had evidently never learned, and Fargo was glad he hadn't. For as Lester issued his threat, Fargo lanced the rigid fingers of his free hand into Lester's eyes. Lester automatically let go and covered his eyes with both hands.

Fargo had Genritt right where he wanted him. He drew back the toothpick for a fatal thrust, then hesitated. To his utter amazement, Lester had commenced to bawl like a baby. His blade wavered. With an abrupt gesture he switched it from his right hand to his left, balled his right fist, and powered his arm into an uppercut that began down around his knees and ended at the point of contact on Lester's jaw.

For a moment nothing happened. Lester stopped bawling, but all he did was stand in mute silence. Then his arms drooped and his legs bent. His massive bulk melted to the floor and was still.

Fargo stared down at the last of the Genritt brothers, his emotions in a whirl. More than anything, he wanted to slay Lester for what Lester had just done. But unbidden into his mind popped the thought that Lester was not entirely in the wrong.

Desma and he had been trespassing on Genritt property when Lester and Silly Boy caught them. The brothers had not known that Morco and Buck had stolen Fargo's horse. Lester and Silly Boy had every right to march Desma and him up to their parents to find out what to do with them. For that reason, and that reason alone, Fargo had not shot them dead. He had deliberately wounded Silly Boy in the shoulder and contented himself with knocking Lester out.

And now? It upset Fargo to realize that Silly Boy and Lester had never seen their brothers with the Ovaro. They had no idea what Buck and Morco had done. Lester and Silly Boy had tracked him down to avenge what they saw as the baseless murders of their kin.

Fargo reluctantly inserted the toothpick into its ankle sheath. Retrieving his rifle and pistol, he went to the bar, filled a glass to the brim with whiskey, and swallowed the coffin varnish in a single gulp. The warmth in his gut invigorated him. Wiping his mouth with his sleeve, he stepped back down the hall, over Lester, to the rear doorway.

The bright sunlight made him squint. Fargo shoved the Henry into the scabbard, climbed on the stallion, and rode to the front of the building. About to turn, he drew rein at a noise and whipped around, the Colt gleaming in his hand.

The hog had reappeared. It stood over Luke Genritt, greedily chomping on the flesh of Silly Boy's face and neck, grisly pieces dangling from its mouth, its snout speckled red. It looked up and grunted.

Fargo killed it. One shot to the head was all it took. The hog staggered against the store, its dull eyes growing duller. Its short legs collapsed, spilling it onto the earth beside the man it had been about to eat.

Possum Hollow was still as empty as a graveyard at midnight. Not a single soul had ventured outdoors to learn what the shooting was about. Not a single person seemed to care what happened to Big Bob or the Genritt brothers.

Fargo was glad to be shed of the place. He headed to the northeast at a trot. On coming to rank swampland, he slowed to a walk. The trail meandered this way and that through dense growth and past deep pools where alligators lurked.

It was unfortunate that Big Bob had not supplied better directions before he died. Trying to find a single cabin in the middle of the vast bayou country was a lot like searching for the proverbial needle in a haystack. Fargo did know that the abandoned homestead was supposed to be approximately six miles from Possum Hollow, which narrowed the area down. But it was still a challenge.

About five miles from the town, Fargo came on a network of game trails. A few bore human tracks, as well. He followed one until it petered out at the edge of a gator-infested channel. Another took him into briars so thick no living animal could have gone through them without being torn to ribbons.

The sun was high in the afternoon sky when Fargo turned a bend, and in front of him was a trail wider than the rest. Better yet, it bore the freshest footprints, some having been made that very morning. He followed its winding course to a spine of land that reared up out of the swamp like the jagged backbone of a gigantic beast.

The crack of a shot brought Fargo to a stop. There was another, and another. Whoever was firing was not shooting at him, so at length he rode on. Leaving the trail, he worked cautiously up the ridge. More shots drowned out the steady drone of insects. Someone laughed. Someone else cursed.

In a cypress stand Fargo ground-hitched the Ovaro. Gliding from cover to cover, he presently came to a wide basin.

It looked as if part of the slope had buckled ages ago. In the center stood a cabin more decrepit than any he had yet seen. A section of the roof was missing, and the west wall sagged. Part of the chimney had fallen away.

Four men were out front. Two had been with Henri Lacombe when Fargo encountered the Cajun before. Empty whiskey bottles had been set up at one end of the clearing, and they were taking turns breaking them. As Fargo looked on, a beefy cutthroat in ragged clothes took aim and broke one of the bottles neatly in two. The man spat a wad of tobacco, then sneered at his companions.

"Your turn, Pritchard. Try not to miss this time."

Pritchard was the smallest. Sporting a beard that covered half his chest, he lifted a rifle and took forever to sight down it. At the blast, a chunk of the log on which the bottles had been placed flew into the air, but the bottles remained intact.

The others laughed. Swearing lustily, Pritchard reloaded. "Mock me all you want," he grumbled, "but I never claimed to be much of a marksman." He patted a long knife on his left hip. "It's the blade I'm good with, and don't none of you ever forget it."

"Simmer down, you feisty runt," the beefy man said. "This is all in fun. There's no need for you to be takin' everything so personal."

"I'll do as I damn well please, Torrance," Pritchard argued. "And don't call me a runt again or I'll carve your black heart out and feed it to the gators."

Torrance glared. "Why, you little jackass. I could lick you with one hand." He spat tobacco juice at Pritchard's feet and the small ruffian danced aside.

"I warned you!" Pritchard said, snaking out his knife in a fluid swing at the bigger man's loins. Torrance barely stepped back in time. "I'm tired of you always riding me. It's time you learned that you can't treat people like dirt and get away with it."

The other two men hastily moved out of the way as Torrance drew his own knife and circled Pritchard. The bitterness of their rivalry was reflected by the hatred in their faces.

Before the pair could clash, a new figure in a long dark coat strode from the cabin. Folding his arms, he stared at Pritchard and Torrance. Instantly they lowered their blades and straightened. "Isn't this just wonderful, *mes amis*? I leave you alone for five minutes and you behave like *enfants*."

"Sorry, Lacombe. It won't happen again," Torrance said.

"Yeah, boss," Pritchard confirmed. "Things just got a little out of hand, is all."

Henri Lacombe stepped off the porch and over to Pritchard. His right arm slowly extended. He gave it a slight twist and suddenly a glittering blade was in his hand, the tip jabbing into the small man's cheek. "Is that a fact, Charles?" Lacombe's voice was tempered steel itself. "I heard you braggin' about your skill. Maybe you would like to try it against mine, eh? Then you can be the boss if you win."

Pritchard was scared, and it showed. Swallowing hard, he went to shake his head, stiffening when the blade tip gouged deeper. "I'd never try to take your place, Henri. You know that. None of us would be that crazy."

The Cajun pursed his lips, gave his arm another twist, and stepped back. The blade had disappeared as if by magic. "I weary of your childish antics. Either listen to me from now on or suffer the consequences."

Torrance was fumbling with his knife, attempting to slip it back into its sheath without drawing attention to himself. He failed.

Lacombe walked up to him and plucked the weapon from Torrance's fingers. "Havin' trouble, are you?" Suddenly reversing his grip, Lacombe spun and threw the knife overhand. It thudded into a porch post, dead center.

Fargo was impressed. The four underlings were vicious cutthroats in their own right, bravos who had undoubtedly killed more than a few men in their time. In any saloon brawl they could more than hold their own. Yet they were terrified of the Cajun, treating him as a rattler that might strike at any moment. Lacombe had to be twice as vicious as they were, and twice as skilled, to instill such fear.

The Cajun returned to the cabin, saying over a shoulder, "I do not care to be disturbed again, *mes amis*. I trust you will not disappoint me, eh?"

The four men moved to the log and sat. One produced a flask, which was passed around.

Fargo flattened. Now that he had found the Cajun, what next? It wouldn't do to walk on in there and demand to know what had happened to Jasmine Tanner. In the gunfight that was bound to result, the Cajun might be killed, and for all Fargo knew, Lacombe was the only one who could reveal her fate. The best course seemed to be to lie low, wait for a chance to jump Lacombe when the others were not around, and force the Cajun to tell him.

The afternoon waned. The four men on the log finished off the flask. Wilson, the hothead who had nearly charged Fargo when Fargo told them to strip off their pants and boots the day before, broke out a deck of cards. Pritchard sat by himself at one end, whittling on a stick.

All was quiet and peaceful until an angry shout rose from the cabin. Fargo heard Lacombe swear lustily, heard a ringing slap. The Cajun reappeared, only this time he was not alone. In his grip struggled the brunette Fargo thought that he had saved from them. Her cheek was red from the slap. She cried out when Lacombe pushed her. Her foot caught in a chink in the boards, and she sprawled onto her hands and knees. Gamely she made as if to flee, but Lacombe was on her in a heartbeat, his fingers wrapped in her lustrous hair.

Torrance, Pritchard, Wilson, and the last member of the

gang came over on the run. "What happened, Henri?" asked the former.

"The bitch bit me," Lacombe fumed, touching his right ear, where blood tickled onto his neck. "She bit me!" he repeated, as if he could not quite believe it. Growling, he struck the brunette across the mouth, knocking her down. Then something snapped inside of him. His ruggedly handsome features contorted into a feral mask. Stomping on the woman's arm to pin her, he flailed away at her head, her shoulders, her sides. She screeched. She pleaded with him to stop. But it did her no good. The Cajun had gone berserk. He beat her brutally, swatting her arms aside when she tried to protect herself.

Now Fargo saw firsthand why the other cutthroats were afraid of Lacombe. The man was a walking volcano that could erupt at any time. If someone did not act, the Cajun was going to beat that poor woman to death.

Even though Lacombe was his only link to Jasmine, Fargo trained the Henry on Lacombe's chest. He tried not to think of how devastated little Jessica would be if he failed to locate her older sister. It could not be helped.

Unexpectedly Torrance and Wilson leaped in close and grabbed Lacombe's arms. The Cajun roared, shaking Wilson off. At that point all of them piled on, holding onto his arms and legs so he could not strike them or employ his hidden blade. Gradually Lacombe calmed down. The color faded from his face. He quit growling and sucked in a deep breath.

"I am fine now. You can let me go."

Torrance was not so certain. "Are you sure? We know how you get when you're like this. The last time, you carved up that river man in New Orleans. Remember?"

Lacombe straightened. "I said I am fine," he insisted.

"No hard feelings, boss?" Pritchard asked. "You told us yourself that no harm was to come to her, that she's worth five hundred, easy."

"*Let me go.*" The words were clipped and precise, fired like bullets. The four hardcases did as they were told but they were not happy about it. All four contrived to place their hands near their hardware, afraid their leader would turn on them.

Henri Lacombe tucked in his shirt and adjusted his coat. "My apologies, gentlemen," he said formally. "I fault you for actin' up, then I do the same thing. Slivers and planks, eh?"

"Huh?" Wilson said.

"Nevermind," Lacombe responded. "I keep forgettin' that none of you can read." Wheeling, he entered the cabin and shortly emerged carrying a rope. Without a word of explanation, he walked to a tree bordering the clearing and tossed one end over a branch ten feet above him. Catching it, he made a loop. "Bring Ada here," he commanded.

Torrance and Wilson did the honors. Their captive bore bruises on her arms and had a welt on her cheek, but otherwise she appeared unharmed by the Cajun's tantrum. Holding her chin high and proud, she gazed defiantly at Lacombe.

"This is what I get for trustin' you, for thinkin' that you are a man of honor. My mother was right about you all along. You are filth!"

Lacombe laughed. "Cast all the stones you want, *chérie*. In four days you will not have half the spirit you do now. De Cade will break you, just as he has broken all the rest."

"Never!" Ada exclaimed. "I would rather die than let this go on."

The Cajun laughed harder and winked at Torrance. "It is amusin' is it not, that they all say the same thing? They all cling to what little virtue they have, as if it were their most prized possession." Squatting, he said, "Bring her closer and hold her so she cannot use her legs."

Pritchard and the last man had to help. Ada resisted as best she could, throwing herself from side to side and at-

78

tempting to kick her abductors, but she could not prevent Lacombe from slipping the noose over her feet and tightening it around her ankles. He jumped back as she rammed her knees at his face.

"Nice try, woman," Lacombe taunted. He had the other end of the rope in both hands. Bunching his shoulders, he pulled, spilling her feet out from under her. His henchmen cackled as she was slowly hoisted into the air, her dress sliding down to expose her underthings. The laughter died.

"Help me," Lacombe said. "She should be on a diet." With their assistance, he raised her several feet off the ground, then secured the rope around the trunk so it would not slip. Rubbing his hands, he admired his handiwork. "What nice legs you have, pretty one. They are your most attractive feature, I think."

Ada was rotating from side to side. Helplessness and fury fought for dominance, and fury won. "Let me go, damn you! You have no right to do this!"

"What do rights have to do with anything?" Lacombe retorted. "In this life, *chérie*, the strong ones like me do as they please and the weak ones, like you, do as you are told." He touched his ear. "It would have been better for you if you had let me have my way in there. Now you will hang out here all night. No one will feed you. No one will give you water. By morning you will be cold and hungry and so tired that you will give us no trouble when we start out." He patted her, beckoned his men, and went into the cabin.

Ada's plight changed everything. Fargo watched her struggle to rise high enough to reach the knots. Time and again she made the effort. Time and again she fell back in frustration. After a while her eyes misted, but she bit her lower lip and fought back the tears.

The sun dipped to the horizon and began to sink from sight. Legions of frogs took to croaking, crickets by the thousands chimed in. A few alligators bellowed, and soon dozens were doing so.

From the cabin came low voices and laughter. Clearly at one point rose Trench's, saying, "I'll see your two dollars and raise you two more, runt." They were playing poker.

Fargo crawled toward the tree, never taking his eyes off the cabin for more than a few seconds. Ada hung limply, exhausted, too weak to lift her arms up past her shoulders. She was the perfect picture of despair. He had to swing wide around a patch of thornbushes, slowing when a snake wound across his path. Its markings revealed it was a harmless ribbon snake, so he went on.

When he was a yard from the tree, Fargo rose and drew the Arkansas toothpick. So far Ada had not noticed him. He moved nearer to cut the rope, then heard someone whistling.

The cutthroat whose name Fargo did not know had stepped outside and was coming straight toward the tree.

7

Skye Fargo hugged the tree, leaning the Henry against it so his hands would be free. The man's footsteps were furtive, as if he did not want to be caught doing whatever he planned to do.

Ada twisted to see who it was and said angrily, "What do you want, Benton? Did Lacombe send you out to torment me?"

"Hush, woman!" Benton whispered. "One more peep out of you and it'll be your last." He halted in front of her and licked his lips, his eyes devouring her shapely form. "Ever since he strung you up, I couldn't get the sight of you out of my head. I just want a little feel, is all, then I'll leave you be."

"Go away or I will yell for Lacombe. He will be mad if you so much as lay a finger on me."

Benton was a scruffy man whose body and clothes had not seen water and soap in ages. Scratching himself, he drew a Green River knife and wagged it in front of her nose. "I meant what I said. Let me touch you." Benton poked her shoulder, breaking the skin. "If you don't, I'll cut you, so help me."

"I would rather die than be handled by a pig like you."

The lecher's greedy eyes narrowed. "That could be arranged, missy. I could slit your pretty throat, and everyone would think it was Crazy Joe, that old injun who lives off by himself in the middle of the swamp." He shifted the knife so it was close to her neck.

"Lacombe would guess the truth," Ada predicted.

"Maybe that's a chance I'm willing to take." Flicking his tongue out in savory anticipation, Benton reached for her left thigh.

Fargo had circled around the tree while they were talking. When the cutthroat went to grope her, he sprang, wrapping an arm around Benton's throat from behind while simultaneously plunging the Arkansas toothpick between the man's ribs twice in a row. He struck so quickly that Benton was dead on his feet without having any idea of who had slain him. Lowering the disjointed figure, Fargo stepped to the tree, gripped the rope firmly, and sliced.

"You again!" Ada blurted, and then threw her arms over her head to cushion the impact as gravity took over.

Fargo grabbed the rope with both hands as it parted, arresting her descent before she could hit. Slowly lowering her the rest of the way, he swiftly undid the knots. As he helped her to her feet, she sagged against him, momentarily weak.

"Oh. I'm so dizzy." Ada closed her eyes, her chin drooping.

"It will pass," Fargo said, hustling her toward the undergrowth. He paused to replace his throwing knife and to claim the Henry. Then, when he had her one step from the vegetation and safety, an irate shout spoiled everything.

"Henri! Torrance! Come quick! It's that same feller as before! He's kilt Benton, and he's stealin' the woman!"

Wilson dashed from the porch, unlimbering a revolver from under his belt. The front sight somehow snagged on his pants, and he tugged to get it loose.

Hickok only had one arm free. But the Henry already had a round in the chamber. Raising it, he cocked the hammer, steadied the heavy rifle as best he was able, and fired. The recoil was considerable, though not enough to tear the rifle from his grasp. He saw Wilson catapult backward, then whirled and dashed into the trees.

Ada gained strength with every step she took. Within

82

half a minute she shrugged his arm off and said, "I can manage. Just lead the way and I'll be right behind you."

It was well she could manage on her own. Lusty curses and the crash of brush announced that the four killers were hard on their heels. "Spread out!" the Cajun bawled. "I want them found! Fifty extra dollars to whoever who spots them first!"

Fargo changed direction, heading for the Ovaro. He suddenly hunkered in tall weeds when drumming footsteps came toward them. Ada was so close that her shoulder brushed his. She gasped lightly. An ominous shadow had appeared not ten feet away.

It was Torrance, a pair of pistols sweeping from right to left. He peered hard into the growth, frowned, and moved on. Off to the east someone else was moving through the woods with all the stealth of an enraged bull buffalo.

Waiting a suitable interval, Fargo clasped Ada's warm hand and hurried on. She surprised him by making as little noise as he did. He had to remember that, like Desma, Ada had probably been born and bred in the bayou country. She was more at home in the wilderness than she would be on the streets of a big city. It was another reminder that country girls, as they were called, should never be taken lightly. They were as tough and competent as any man.

Presently the cypress stand came into sight. Fargo could hear one of the cutthroats quite a way to the east, but he did not know where the other two were. He guided Ada in among the towering trees and over to the stallion. The Ovaro had its head high, its ears erect. "Steady, boy," Fargo said, patting its neck. "It's just me and a friend."

But Fargo was wrong. For as he cupped his hands to boost Ada into the saddle, a beefy form moved into the open and trained a pair of Smith and Wessons on him. "That's far enough, mister. Raise your arms and pretend you're a statue or I'll cut you down where you stand." Torrance came toward them, grinning in triumph.

Fargo had been careless. Upset with himself, he hoisted his hands.

"I'm in your debt, friend," Torrance said sarcastically. "I can use that fifty dollars Lacombe promised. They about cleaned me out at cards."

Neither of them was paying much attention to Ada, who suddenly clawed her fingers and leaped at the cutthroat. "*Not again!* I won't let that cur paw me ever again!"

Torrance was taken aback. He pointed a pistol at her but did not fire, perhaps because he did not care to risk Lacombe's wrath. Retreating a step, he exclaimed, "Back off, damn you!"

Ada did not listen. She lit into the gunman like a female wildcat, her nails raking his face and neck. Torrance shoved but she clung on, driving him back against a tree. He yelped when she nearly took out an eye, then struck her across the jaw with a forearm.

"Stop it, you hellion!"

Fargo had been completely forgotten. Darting to the right, he skinned the Colt but he could not fire. Ada was in the road. He shifted, with the same result. She was so intent on clawing out Torrance's eyes that she did not realize the blunder she was making.

Torrance did, though. He spotted Fargo and suddenly hooked an elbow over Ada's left arm, locking her body to his, keeping her between him and Fargo as he wheeled from side to side so that Fargo would not have a clear shot. At the same time, Torrance hauled Ada to the rear, toward the undergrowth.

Sliding farther to the right, Fargo saw an opening. For a few seconds part of Torrance's chest was exposed. He took aim, then had to ease up on the trigger as Ada's body swung into the line of fire once more. Torrance grinned, still backing off, now only a few feet from losing himself and his captive in the growth.

Fargo snapped the Colt out and sighted carefully at the

side of Torrance's head. The wily gunman hunched down, laughing to rub it in.

As if that were not bad enough, from two different points on the ridge arose the crack and snap of breaking twigs and limbs. The Cajun and Pritchard were on their way.

Ordinarily Skye Fargo would never endanger the life of an innocent. But this time he had to in order to save her. Adopting a two-handed grip, he aligned the Colt on the back of Ada's head, holding it there as she bobbed and weaved in her frenzied but futile effort to hurt Torrance. The foliage was closing around them when she shifted and jerked on her trapped arm. For a heartbeat Torrance's face was in plain view. Fargo stroked the trigger.

The gunman's head slammed back. Lifeless, he turned to molten wax, keeling forward, nearly knocking Ada over on his way down. She wrenched her arm out and jumped clear.

The sound of the approaching killers was loud in Fargo's ears as he gripped her wrist and flung her toward the stallion. In moments they were mounted. Applying his spurs and lashing the reins, Fargo goaded the pinto into a headlong gallop down the slope. None too soon.

Henri Lacombe and Pritchard spilled into the open. They cut loose, pistols hammering, lead zinging fast and furious into the trees on either side of the Ovaro. Fargo did not return their fire. He had his hands full, avoiding obstacles. Worrying that Ada might take a bullet meant for him, he angled past a wide oak that afforded extra protection from the deadly hail.

The gunfire ceased about the time the stallion reached the flatland below. Fargo fled along the same trail that had brought him to the cabin. It was ten minutes before he slowed to a walk, another ten before he reined up to look back.

Tears of joy glistened in Ada's eyes. Clamping him tighter, she planted a grateful kiss smack on his mouth.

"You did it, mister! You saved me a second time! I can never thank you enough!"

Fargo trotted on. "We're not out of the woods yet," he noted. "Lacombe might come after you."

"Let him. He doesn't have a horse. He'll never catch up." Ada rested her cheek on his shoulder, her voice softening. "I thought for sure I'd never see my family again. Lacombe has been stealin' women from hereabouts for months now."

"I know," Fargo said. "I'm a friend of Desma Collinder's and the Tanner family."

"You are?" Ada declared, and launched into a story similar to Jasmine's and Desma's. Lacombe had showed up at her father's cabin one day and expressed his intention to court her. Ada had made it clear that she wanted nothing to do with him, and he had left. Days later he had shown up again, the first of many visits he paid. Initially he was friendly, working his charm, confident she would give in and go with him willingly. When it became apparent that he was wasting his time, Lacombe had threatened her, then tried to abduct her. That was when Fargo had stumbled on the cutthroats the first time and saved her. Temporarily, at any rate.

"Last night I was on my way to the spring when they jumped me," Ada divulged. "Stuck a sack over my head to keep anyone from hearin' my cries and dragged me off into the swamp."

"Which way is your father's place?" Fargo asked. Seeing her safely home would take precious time, but he could not simply leave her there in the middle of nowhere. Lacombe had to wait.

Ada pointed, saying, "I'll give you directions as we go." She craned forward to see his face. "You're welcome to stay the night if you'd like. My ma will be happy to set an extra plate out. And Pa will be so tickled, he'll break out his private jug."

Any other time, Fargo would have gladly accepted her offer. Now he had Jasmine to think of. "I wish I could," he confessed, then inquired, "Do you know what Lacombe had planned for you? Why has he been kidnapping young women?"

"He never said," Ada responded. "It's as much a mystery to me now as it ever was. And believe me, I tried to find out. I pestered him with questions, but he was too sly for me. He would never give me a straight answer." She paused, growing thoughtful. "He did let a couple of things slip, though."

"Such as?"

"I overheard him tell Torrance that he wanted to be ready to leave for Baton Rouge at daybreak. Later, when Wilson and Pritchard were complainin' about not getting all the money due them, Lacombe told them not to worry, that Jace De Cade was as good as his word and they would all be paid on their next trip in."

"Jace De Cade," Fargo said. Now he had somewhere to start hunting for Jasmine and a name linked to her disappearance. "Do you know who De Cade is?"

"Never heard of the man." Ada was quiet awhile. "Mr. Fargo, are you thinkin' of going up against these people?"

"I promised Jessie I'd find her sister. I won't rest until I do."

"Then, you'll be headin' for Baton Rouge," Ada said. "I know a man there who can help you. He knows the capital well since he's lived there going on twenty years. He's a friend of my pa's by the name of Louis Caddo. He's a Cajun, too, but he is nothin' like Lacombe. Ask for him at the Brown Pelican Tavern."

"I may take you up on that."

It only took two hours to reach the homestead. Fargo halted at the edge of the clearing and helped Ada off. She held onto his hand, lingering, loathe to have him leave. "I do wish you'd reconsider. It's not safe ridin' in the swamps at night. Stay until morning. I can guarantee you will be very well treated."

Her request implied an invitation Fargo found hard to refuse, yet he did. The Cajun had probably already gone. But he had to get back. Bending, he kissed Ada's forehead. "Another time, maybe," he said, and left, his last sight of her as she waved longingly and blew him a kiss of her own.

Only the fact that Fargo had a knack for memorizing landmarks enabled him to find his way to the spine of land in the dead of night. It was nerve-racking, riding along with alligators bellowing on every side, with the vegetation constantly rustling and the grass shaking and swaying to the passage of unseen creatures. Loud and not so loud splashes showed that the water was alive with wild things. Frequently the stark cries of prey caught in the grip of hungry predators would cause the bayou to fall silent, but only for a short while. Soon the swamp would crawl once more with moving things, the cycle of life and death being replayed again and again and again.

By Fargo's reckoning it was close to midnight when he reached the west end of the jagged ridge. On foot, leading the stallion, he climbed until he was northwest of the basin. A convenient narrow shelf gave him the perfect spot to spy on the cabin. Through a window on the side gleamed the yellow glow of a lantern. Lacombe and Pritchard were still there. They must have assumed he would not be back until morning.

Seated with his back to a log, Fargo allowed himself to doze. The night passed uneventfully except for two times when he was awakened. Once, by a hideous bleating to the southwest that went on and on until it was strangled off. The second incident came when something scuttled across the log behind him. Springing up, he spun, but whatever it was had been just as startled and hurtled into thick grass.

From then until pink streaks brightened the eastern horizon, Fargo slept fitfully. Stretching, he rose and headed into the basin, approaching the cabin from the rear. A steep earthen bank had to be negotiated. As he squatted to slide down, loose dirt cascaded to the bottom. It made enough noise to be heard inside, so Fargo threw caution to the wind and flew down.

Running to the window, Fargo ducked under it and listened. No sounds at all came from inside. Darting around the corner, he rammed his shoulder at the door. It gave way with no problem, creaking noisily, and he moved to the left so his silhouette would not be framed in the doorway.

He need not have bothered. The cabin was empty. On a small table sat the lantern, which had burned itself out, and a partial sheet of paper.

The paper was old and yellow and frayed. In pencil someone had written, "*I knew you would come back, meddler. So I left the lantern on for you.*"

Fargo crumpled the note and hurled it to the floor. Lacombe had made a fool of him. The Cajun had left the lantern on to trick him into thinking they were still there when actually Lacombe and Pritchard had left the preceding evening. By now they were well on their way.

Other than the table, the only furniture was a broken bed and two chairs that had been recently patched together. Fargo looked under the bed and scoured the floor, but came up with no additional clues.

Since there was nothing to be gained by staying in the cabin, Fargo swung onto the Ovaro and went completely around it. The sign he sought bore to the northeast. He had visions of riding long and hard and overtaking the Cajun before nightfall, but the tracks ended at the swamp. Lacombe and Pritchard had waded into deep water to throw him off their scent.

Fargo was not disturbed by it. He knew where the pair were heading, so he bent the stallion's hooves toward Baton Rouge. That night he camped out under the stars on a barren hill. The next he spent in an old barn. On the morning of the third day he crested a rise and beheld the muddy Mississippi in the distance. Above the river rose the bluffs on which the capital had been built.

Baton Rouge meant "red stick" in French. It had been established by them over a hundred and forty years ago, but only within the past decade had it been picked to be Louisiana's capital.

Some thought New Orleans was a better choice. It had more people and was closer to the Gulf of Mexico. But Baton Rouge won out and since then had been growing by leaps and bounds. A rowdy mix of settlers with French, Spanish, and English roots mingled with Creoles and Cajuns and ruffians of every stripe. Farmers and river men, trappers and hunters, city dandies and gruff backwoodsmen, all made life in Baton Rouge colorful. As well as dangerous.

Brawls and knife fights were common. The use of pistols was strongly frowned on by local authorities. Duels were still fought, but in isolated spots where the squeamish would not be offended.

As Fargo scaled the bluffs, he gazed out over the broad Mississippi. The river was being piled by a variety of vessels. Barges laden with goods, riverboats, both double-engine side-wheelers and single-engine stern-wheelers, keelboats and pleasure craft, ships in from the ocean, they filled the waterway for as far as the eye could see.

Just below Fargo a snag boat was at work. Double-hulled vessels, they were designed to latch onto partially sunken trees and remove them by means of a windlass. Snags were a constant threat to navigation thanks to floods and erosion along the riverbanks. They caused two-thirds of all the wrecks on the Mississippi, costing dozens of lives and untold thousands in lost merchandise every year.

The city bustled with as much activity as the river. Fargo shared the road with countless riders, wagons, carriages, coaches, and drays. Since buckskins were favored by many of the muskrat trappers who came to Baton Rouge daily to sell their hides, as well as by a lot of the backwoodsmen and river men, he did not stand out as he would have done in a city farther east.

Fargo started asking around about the Brown Pelican. From a party of river men he learned that it was on the waterfront, in a seedy district shunned by members of polite society. Shortly after noon, he drew rein in front of the squat building and stiffly dismounted. After two and a half days in the saddle, he was in need of hot food and a drink or three.

The interior was as gloomy as a cave. Fargo stood just inside the door until his eyes adjusted, then crossed to a bar. It was early yet, so few patrons were evident. At a table sat three men playing cards. In the corner a woman in a red dress and a young gentleman friend were nose to nose. At the bar were two Creoles.

A lean man wearing the baggy shirt and woolen pants typical of river men tended bar. A blue cap crowned his thatch of brown and gray hair at a rakish angle. On his chin was a tiny scar. His eyes were the color of his cap, and they regarded Fargo with casual interest. "What can I do for you, *monsieur*?" he asked in a heavy accent that showed his ancestors hailed from France.

"Food and drink for a start," Fargo said, pushing his hat back. "Information, too. I'm looking for someone."

The bartender sniffed. "Food and drink we give you, *monsieur*. As for the rest, I know nothin' about no one. *Comprenez-vous*?"

"It's not what you think. I need to find a man named Louis Caddo. A friend of his told me that this was the place to ask for him."

"I know no one by that name. Maybe this friend tell you wrong, *monsieur*."

Fargo glanced at the Creoles to ask them but the pair picked up their drinks and walked to a table. He hadn't been back in Baton Rouge an hour and already he was feeling as welcome as he had in Possum Hollow. From a menu posted on the wall he ordered his meal, then took a seat.

The scent of the bouillabaisse set before him made his mouth water. Since the soup hardly whetted his appetite, he had a heaping plate of catfish, half a loaf of bread, and black coffee flavored with the root of the chicory plant.

The barman brought him a glass of whiskey, and Fargo had him leave the bottle, saying, "Have you changed your mind about telling me where to find Caddo? It's important that I do."

"What makes you think I know him, eh?" The man's English was slurred, as if he had never made a whole-hearted effort to master it.

"The person who told me about him wouldn't lie," Fargo explained. He would have gone into detail, but the man walked off. Sighing, he drank a third of the bottle, just enough to take the stiffness out of his joints and put him in good spirits. A Spanish woman came out of the back to take his money. He tried asking her about Caddo but she shook her head, refusing to say a word.

Fargo had not been born the day before. He was not surprised in the least when he stepped outside and heard a pistol hammer click. At the corner of the tavern stood the barman with a leveled derringer. Flanking him, as somber as hangmen, were the Creoles.

"Now, *monsieur*, you tell me about this friend of yours. And I hope, for your sake, it be someone I know."

8

Skye Fargo made no attempt to draw his pistol. He regarded the trio as soberly as they regarded him, saying, "Why not just admit who you are, Caddo? Why pretend you've never heard of yourself? Is the law after you?"

Louis Caddo shook his head. "But I make more than a few enemies in my time, *monsieur*. Any man who is a man does." The derringer he held was a three-barreled gun manufactured by the Marston company. He moved around so that his back was to the street and passers-by would not notice it. "I am waiting."

"Ada Beidler told me about you," Fargo explained. Briefly he related her abduction at the hands of Lacombe and mentioned that other young women had disappeared. By the time he was done, Caddo had lowered the derringer. At a nod from the Cajun, the Creoles melted into the flow of pedestrians.

"Henri Lacombe," Caddo said, as if pronouncing the name of a disease. "He is well-known in Baton Rouge. A devil, that one. His tongue is forked, as the Indians say. Not a man to take lightly."

"Where can I find him?"

Louis Caddo slid the derringer into a pocket. "I wish I could tell you. He and I, we do not move in the same circles. But I hear of him a lot. He is in many knife fights, that one. He has killed dozens."

Yet another reason why Torrance and the others had been so afraid of him, Fargo mused. "There is another man involved. Have you ever heard the name Jace De Cade?"

The Cajun's eyes widened, and he whistled loudly. "De Cade? *Monsieur*, that is very bad. He is a big man in Baton Rouge. Very rich. With much influence." He scanned the Mississippi, concentrating on the docks. "I do not see it."

"See what?"

"De Cade has a boat. The *River Queen*, she is called. She is a beauty, a side-wheeler, one of the largest anywhere. And so elegant! He keeps her busy going back and forth from Baton Rouge to New Orleans."

Fargo had been on riverboats before so he could imagine what the vessel must be like. It added to the mystery. What possible link could there be between the shiftless Lacombe and a man as incredibly wealthy as Jace De Cade? He voiced the question aloud.

"There you have me," Caddo said. "They are worlds apart, those two. The only things Lacombe is good at is stealin' and killin'. De Cade has no need to steal, and if he needs killin' done, he can always have his own men do it. He has no need for a fox like Lacombe."

More curious by the day, Fargo noted. "Will you help me find out what Lacombe is up to?" he bluntly asked.

The Cajun pondered a few moments. "For sweet Ada, yes. I will do what I can. But I must warn you." As if they had been the best of friends for years, he draped an arm over Fargo's shoulder, then said in a low tone so no one else could possibly hear. "Our lives are forfeit if we are not careful. Lacombe has many friends in all the wrong places. *Comprenez-vous?*"

"I understand," Fargo assured him.

"Good!" Caddo clapped Fargo on the back. "Come inside, *mon ami*. Rest. Drink. Tell me more about Ada and her father. Tonight we begin the hunt. And let us hope the quarry does not learn we are huntin' them." Caddo steered them toward the door. "It is claimed that there are more bones on the bottom of the Mississippi than in the graveyards. I do not know about you. But I do not want mine to be among them."

On that cheerful note Fargo entered the Brown Pelican. The two of them talked for over an hour. Then he left to take the Ovaro to the nearest livery. Returning, Caddo permitted him to lie down on a cot in a back room and catch some sleep before the sun went down. Once it did, the search commenced.

Ada had been right about the Cajun. He knew Baton Rouge from end to end. He was familiar with every tavern, saloon, and grogshop in the city. He had contacts everywhere, and the two of them spent the next several hours making the rounds, asking about Henri Lacombe everywhere they went.

Fargo admired how Caddo handled himself. The Cajun never let on why he was interested in Lacombe or said anything that would arouse undue suspicion. No, Caddo's favorite tactic was to engage an acquaintance in idle talk, then casually say, "Oh, by the way. Have you heard about the knife fight Henri Lacombe was in the other day?"

Of course, there had not been one. It was Caddo's way of duping the others into talking about Lacombe, and it worked every time.

Shortly after ten, as they stepped from a grogshop that had reeked of spilled grog and human sweat, Caddo frowned and said gloomily, "It is not going well, my friend. As I told you, Lacombe is not an easy one to track down."

"Where to next?" Fargo asked.

Caddo nodded at a tavern set close to the water's edge. Moored to the north and south of it were steamboats, flatboats, and packets. "The Mad Piper. It is owned by a Scotsman named O'Hagan. He was a top navigator until he lost a leg in a crash." Caddo patted the pocket where he kept the derringer. "But his is not a place for the timid. Stay close to me, friend. Let me do the talkin'."

Cigar and cigarette smoke was as thick as fog. Every table was occupied, the open spaces crammed. It was by far the most crowded establishment they had been in. River men of every stripe were there. Caddo moved among them smiling and laughing and nodding to men he knew. A few of the patrons cast narrowed looks at Fargo but glanced away when they saw who he was with.

Fargo was halfway across the room when he realized that he was the only one there who was not a river man. The Mad Piper was one of their favorite haunts, as exclusive as the lavish clubs for the rich situated higher on the bluffs.

Louis Caddo bellied up to the bar, shook hands with a grizzled customer, then pounded the counter and bawled, "We'd like service here, you Scottish misfit! Service, I say!"

The man dispensing drinks was heavyset and florid. A full beard framed a friendly face. He clumped over, his peg leg thumping the floorboard in regular cadence. "Well, bless me if it isn't Caddo himself!" beamed the owner. "And here I thought you were dead and buried, it's been so long since last you graced these premises."

Fargo watched the two shake hands. He leaned on the bar and swatted at a cloud of pipe smoke that threatened to engulf him. A chair scraped off to the left, but he did not think much of it.

Caddo introduced O'Hagan, adding with a twinkle in his eyes, "He is one of the few men I would trust with my life. As honest as the day is long, as the sayin' goes."

The Scotsman chuckled. "My blushes, boyo! As for my honesty, I have my sainted mother to thank. 'Always be the proper gentleman,' she was forever saying. Damn me if it didn't sink in, though."

About then a shadow fell across Fargo. He shifted and stared into the beady eyes of a river man bigger than Lester Genritt had been, a bear of a bruiser whose scarred features testified to his ferocity. "You're standing in my spot, farmer," he said in undisguised contempt.

Fargo did not want to cause trouble if he could help it. Tracking down Jasmine was more important than his pride.

Stepping to the right to make room, he replied, "There's plenty of space for everyone."

The walking mountain moved in front of him again. "That's my spot, too, farmer." Behind him several men laughed harshly. "It's rude to be taking a man's spot like you're doing. Someone should teach you some manners."

Fargo held his temper in check. The river man was spoiling for a fight, and he was inclined to oblige, but it would not do to cause a ruckus. It might ruin any chances Caddo had of learning the whereabouts of Henri Lacombe. "Where isn't your spot?" he responded.

The river man made a show of studying the floor from one side to the other. "Know what? Now that I think about it, there isn't a spot here that isn't mine. I guess you'll just have to leave while you still have teeth."

O'Hagan suddenly appeared at Fargo's elbow. "Here, here! What's all this, then? I won't abide troublemakers, Larson. You know that. So sheathe your claws, boyo. You and your bunch go back to your game of cards."

Larson wagged a thick finger. "I don't like anyone telling me what to do, Scotsman." His finger flicked out to jab Fargo's chest. "And I don't like yacks who have no business being here. This buckskin dandy isn't one of us. Show him the door or I'll do it for you."

"This is my establishment," O'Hagan answered angrily. "I can serve who I damn well please. There is no sign out front saying 'River Men Only.'" He motioned at a table. "Now, sit down and behave yourself or I'll show *you* the door, and it will be the last time you'll ever be allowed in."

Reluctantly Larson and his backers moved off, but they were not pleased about it.

"Don't pay that dullard any mind," O'Hagan said. "Every basket has a few bad apples, and he happens to be one of the baddest of our fraternity. Mostly he's bark and not bite."

Caddo had his hand in the derringer pocket. "Someone should have done the rest of us a favor and shot him long ago." He nudged Fargo. "Don't let him get to you, *mon ami*. In a few minutes we will go, and you can forget all about him."

The Scotsman brought Fargo a drink that he nursed until the Cajun signaled they should leave. Wading through the sea of smoke, Fargo was last out the door. He inhaled the cool air gratefully, inquiring, "Did you learn anything?"

Before Caddo could reply, two men sprang out of the darkness and seized him by the arms. Fargo's right hand dived for the Colt, but a sharp object poked into the small of his back and a gravel voice said, "Draw that and you're a dead man, farmer. I want you to back up slowly and join me and my friends down by the river. We'd like a few words with you."

Fargo did as the river man wanted. Larson's breath stank of alcohol. It would not take much to set him off. Two more river men joined them, both smiling eagerly.

Caddo struggled in vain. "I resent this outrage!" he protested. "Let us go, you pigs! This man is a friend of mine. You have no business givin' him grief."

"Shut up, Cajun," Larson said. "You should know better than to bring his kind into the Mad Piper. It's for us and ours, not for clods who don't know port from stern." His knife dug a fraction deeper into Fargo's back.

Caddo would not keep quiet. "I warn you. I will take it personally if you hurt him. He has never done any of you any harm."

Larson relieved Fargo of the Colt. "Think I care, Cajun? Your friend just happened to come along when I'm in the mood to pound a head in. It might as well be his as anyone else's."

The Mississippi was tranquil except for the boat traffic, heavy even at night. Their lights shimmered on the surface like fireflies. Tiny wavelets lapped at the shore. The river man prodded Fargo past a quiet steamboat to a stretch of bare earth. "This will do," Larson announced, handing the Colt to another man. His knife went into a belt sheath.

Fargo had run into riffraff like Larson before. In every town and city, it seemed as if there was at least one self-styled tough who took sick delight in inflicting pain on innocents. When bored or in their cups, these bullies went on the prowl for new victims. Strangers, usually. Always someone they thought they could lick with no problem.

Rubbing the acorn-size knuckles of his right hand against the palm of his left, Larson sneered. "This won't take long, farmer. Not if you stand there and take your punishment like a man."

"And what if I don't?" Fargo rejoined, exploding into an uppercut that had all his weight and power behind it. His fist connected with the river man's jaw, jolting Larson backward. Startled, Larson tried to set himself, but Fargo was on him in a bound, landing two blows. The first staggered the river man, the second pitched him into the Mississippi with a tremendous splash.

The other river men were as stunned as Larson had been. None made an attempt to intervene as their leader sputtered to the surface, then slogged onto land dripping wet. He looked up just as Fargo hit him again, a stiff jab to the cheek that spun Larson half around.

"No!" Larson raged, finally defending himself by raising both arms in a boxing posture.

Fargo hardly rated the river man worth the effort. It was plain that Larson relied on size alone in a fight. The man had no skill to speak of, the few punches he threw as Fargo closed in were mistimed and haphazard. Fargo, on the other hand, knew just where to strike and did so, a combination of hooks and straight-armed swings that resulted in Larson sagging to his knees, his mouth puffy, one eye bloody and beginning to swell.

"Enough," Larson said. "I know when I'm beat."

That was the thing about bullies. Once the tide turned against them, they were all too ready to quit or turn tail. Fargo drew back a step, debating whether to let the man off. Then he thought of all those Larson must have abused over the years. "Think of this the next time you get an urge to pick on someone." His right boot arced up, catching Larson under the jaw. Teeth crunched. Larson was flung onto his back and lay still.

Fargo spun. "Anyone else?" he demanded. When no one had a word to say, he claimed the Colt and backed away, Louis Caddo at his side. The Cajun found the whole thing highly amusing.

"You are something, *mon ami*. He did not land a single blow. Not one! When this gets around, I think people will not fear him as much as they have."

Of more interest to Fargo was what Caddo might have learned about Henri Lacombe. He had already put the fight from his mind. It was but one of many, not memorable in any respect. "About the man we're after?" he prodded.

Caddo glanced back to see if they were being followed. "The Scotsman was our best bet, and he knows little. It is rumored that Lacombe and De Cade are linked, but no one knows how. All O'Hagan knew for sure is that Lacombe has been seen going on and off the *River Queen* a lot of late."

"That's all?" Fargo was profoundly disappointed. He'd hoped for a lot more, such as an address where Lacombe could be found when in the city.

"I am sorry," Caddo said. "We will keep searchin', though. The night, she is young yet. Who knows what we will uncover, *monsieur*."

As it turned out, they uncovered nothing new. By two in the morning they had exhausted Caddo's contacts and were on their way back to the Brown Pelican. "What will you do now?" Caddo inquired.

"Wait around for the *River Queen* to show," Fargo said. It was the sole option left to him. Or was it? "You mentioned that De Cade is one of the wealthiest men in the city. He must have other property besides the riverboat."

"Oh, he does," the Cajun confirmed. "He has the grandest estate in all of Louisiana. He also owns businesses. How many, exactly, I cannot say. But I know a hotel that is his, called the Fountain Head. A strange name, that."

"In the morning take me to the hotel," Fargo proposed.

"What do you hope to find there, *mon ami?*"

"I have no idea," Fargo admitted. But it was as good an idea as any other. He had done as Ada suggested and was no closer to finding Jasmine Tanner. Since it might be days before De Cade's steamboat returned, and since he did not care to sit around twiddling his thumbs until then, he had to make the best of the situation. The hotel and the estate were logical starting points.

They got to bed so late that Fargo figured Louis Caddo would sleep in. The Cajun proved him wrong by shaking him awake before sunrise.

"Do you always waste away the whole day? Breakfast will be served in fifteen minutes. If you are late, my wife will not hold food for you."

His wife was the Spanish woman who had handled Fargo's bill the day before. A quiet, painfully shy woman, she did not say two words to him during the entire meal. Fargo filled himself to the brim with cakes and coffee. The sun had been up an hour when Caddo resumed the hunt.

The hotel was in a seedy section of the city, surrounded by grogshops and houses of ill repute. It was three stories high, unusual in Baton Rouge. Over the entrance a sign had been painted in bold black letters: WOMEN'S DOMICILIARY.

The Cajun scratched his head. "Does that mean what I think it means?"

"Ladies only," Fargo verified, mildly surprised. He had heard of hotels exclusively for women, but they were in places like New York City and Boston.

Caddo was just as confounded. "No one told me this. How are we to find her if we can not go inside?"

"It won't hurt to knock and ask." Fargo crossed the rutted excuse for a street and tried the latch on the wide door.

It was locked. He rapped politely, hoping that the woman who answered would not be a stodgy matron whose duty it was to shoo off any and all wolves wanting into the chicken coop. Plastering his best smile on his face, he waited as heavy steps sounded within and the latch rasped.

The door swung inward. Filling the doorway was a man as squat as a bulldog with a countenance to match. Over his left eye hung a black leather patch. Coiled around his right shoulder was a bullwhip. "What do you two want?" he growled.

Fargo glanced at the sign. "I thought only women live here."

"They do. And they need someone to look after them, to make sure that they aren't pestered by the likes of you," the man said. "That's where I come in. I work for the owner. Bullwhip Mulligan is my name. Maybe you've heard of me."

"I have," Louis Caddo said. "You killed a young man last year with that whip of yours. Flayed half his skin off. It was the talk of the city."

Mulligan's square jaw jutted forward. "His name was Jones, and he had it coming. He was molesting a friend of the man I work for. When I went to stop him, the jackass pulled a gun on me." He patted the whip. "I guess the idiot didn't know that I can put out a candle at twenty paces with this beauty." He fixed his baleful eye on Fargo. "Enough chitchat. I've work to do. If you have a reason for bothering me, I'm all ears."

"Jasmine Tanner," Fargo said.

"What about her?"

"I'm told she is staying here," Fargo bluffed. "I've come all the way from Possum Hollow with word from her family, and I'd like to see her."

Bullwhip Mulligan's bald pate creased. "Tanner, you say? I can't recollect as I've heard the name. What makes you think she is staying here, anyway?"

"She works for Jace De Cade, who owns this hotel," Fargo fibbed again in an effort to trick the watchdog into revealing information.

"Mr. De Cade is my boss, sure enough," Mulligan said, "but he doesn't have anything to do with the women who rent rooms here. They're hardly the type he likes to socialize with. Ask anyone." Mulligan stepped back and started to close the door.

"Wait a minute," Fargo said, sticking his foot against the jamb. "Couldn't you at least go look at the register? Maybe she checked in when you weren't around."

"I'm *always* around," Bullwhip Mulligan said. "It's what I'm paid for." He slammed the door so quickly that Fargo barely pulled his foot out in time. A bolt was thrown, and Mulligan tromped off, muttering.

"Friendly soul, *n'est-ce pas*?" the Cajun said. "They say that he practices by taking the heads off baby ducks down by the river. His eye was lost in a saloon brawl. The one who did it lost four fingers and part of his lower lip."

Fargo went back across the street, bothered by what they had learned. Why would an influential man like De Cade have a brutal character like Mulligan working for him? At a domiciliary for women, no less? And why establish a hotel for women at all? It was not as if New Orleans had an abundance of them. As in every city on the frontier, females were in short supply.

"What will you do now?" Caddo wanted to know.

Fargo entered an alley between a tavern and a dry goods store. "I'm going to keep an eye on the hotel for a spell. You can go on with whatever you have to do. I'll meet you at the Brown Pelican about noon."

The Cajun arched a brow at the domiciliary. "Very well. But I hope you know what you are doing. De Cade is not someone I would want for an enemy."

Once Caddo left, the minutes crawled by. Fargo saw several women leave. He toyed with the idea of slipping inside the next time the door opened, but with his luck Mulligan would be the one opening it. Over an hour passed. Then out stepped a young woman with a mane of red hair, just as Jasmine was supposed to have, and a resemblance to Constance in her features. Darting over to intercept her as she headed north up the street, he doffed his hat. "Excuse me, miss. Would your name be Jasmine Tanner?"

The redhead tensed and turned. She eyed him suspiciously, saying, "Do I know you?"

Fargo was all set to explain, to set her at ease, when something whizzed through the air behind him and there was a loud crack. His hat went flying from his hand.

"You don't know how to take a hint, do you, mister?" Bullwhip Mulligan said. "Maybe it's time you learned."

9

Skye Fargo was growing sick and tired of having every hardcase in Louisiana treat him as if it were their natural right to push him around as they saw fit. Slowly rotating, he saw Mulligan holding the bullwhip poised to swing again. Only fifteen feet separated them, and a bullwhip in the hands of a man who knew how to use one was deadly to a distance of twenty-five feet or more depending on the length. Made of braided rawhide, tapering at the end, a bullwhip could peel skin as delicately as a surgeon's scalpel or rip a man wide open like a Bowie.

"I think I'll start with your eyebrows and work my way down," Mulligan declared.

Both of them were caught off guard when the redhead stepped in front of Fargo. "There is no need for violence, Mr. Mulligan," she said. "This man has me confused with someone else, is all." She smiled thinly at Fargo. "No, my name is not Jasmine Tanner. It's Susan Clark. Now, if you will both excuse me—" Nodding at them, she departed rapidly.

Everyone on the street had stopped to stare. Mulligan, glancing around, did not seem to like having so many witness his attack. Slowly lowering the bullwhip, he snapped, "You heard the lady, mister. Maybe now you'll believe that no one called Jasmine Tanner lives here." Backing toward the door, he had one last warning to give. "Don't come around again. The next time will be your last."

The door slammed. Fargo retrieved his hat and examined it for damage. Other than a nick in the crown, it was fine.

Donning it, he grew aware that a curtain covering a lower floor window had parted slightly. He was being spied on. To convince Mulligan that he had learned his lesson, he walked off in the opposite direction the redhead had taken. But at the first block he turned to the left and jogged to the next street. Here he headed north, drawing stares as he ran flat out.

Fargo did not believe the woman had told him the truth. She was the spitting image of how Jasmine was supposed to be. On top of that, there had been a peculiar look in her eyes when she gave her name as Susan Clark, a look that hinted there was more to her than she had let on. He had to find her.

At the second cross street Fargo took another left. Soon he was back on the street the domiciliary was on. Hurrying north, he scanned the pedestrians on both sides for that distinctive mane of red hair and the green dress the woman wore.

Dozens of shops and stores lined both sides. Fargo peered into those he passed. He covered half a mile with no success. Then the streets looped toward the Mississippi. He kept on clear down to the river but never spotted the redhead.

Refusing to give up, Fargo crossed and retraced his route on the other side, checking every establishment where she might have stopped. He did not find her. A block from the domiciliary he halted. For the time being he was thwarted. But he would be back. Later, toward evening, he would hide in the alley and watch until the redhead showed up.

Fargo made for the Cajun's tavern. Along the way he stopped at the livery to check on the Ovaro. A fresh mound of hay in its stall was proof the liveryman was taking good care of it. He stayed long enough to give the pinto a rubdown, then ambled to the Brown Pelican.

The front door, oddly enough, was locked. Fargo had been under the impression that Caddo only kept it bolted from the time the tavern closed until dawn. He walked around to the rear where another door opened into the kitchen. But when he tried this door, it, too, would not budge.

"Louis!" Fargo hollered. No one answered so he tried again. When that failed to garner a reply, he called out the wife's name several times. She did not respond.

The only explanation Fargo could think of was that they had gone off somewhere together. An old bench sat next to the back wall, so he stretched out on it, covered his eyes with his hat, and drifted into a nap that lasted several hours. It was early afternoon when he woke up and stretched.

The back door was still locked. The Caddos had not returned yet. Fargo was mulling what to do when a flatbed wagon appeared and a man in store-bought clothes hopped down and smiled at him. Lifting a box from the bed, the driver came toward the door.

"Howdy, neighbor. I'd be grateful if you'd hold the door for me. I have a delivery to make."

"I would," Fargo said, "but the tavern is locked up. I'm waiting for the Caddos to get back."

The driver scrunched his mouth up. "That's mighty strange. Maria knows this is the day I come. She's always on hand to pay me." He hefted the box. "Well, I suppose I can leave it by the door and she can pay me next time."

That was what he did. After the wagon clattered off, Fargo took his set on the bench and whiled away the time reviewing all that had happened since he first rode into Possum Hollow. It left him no closer to unraveling the truth.

About an hour after the deliveryman was gone, a feeling began to come over Fargo that something was gravely wrong. He glanced at the door, then at the window above the bench. Caddo would have a fit if he broke in for no reason. But on the other hand, he couldn't shake the nagging thought that he should get inside at all costs.

Lying nearby was a fist-size rock. With it in hand, Fargo stepped onto the bench and gave the window a few tentative taps. Looking both ways to be sure no one was observing, he drew back the rock and struck one of the four panes squarely in the center. It shattered nicely. So did the rest, only a few shards left jutting out. These he carefully removed.

Tossing the rock to the ground, Fargo gripped the top of the window and levered himself into it. The fit was tight. He had to wriggle his broad shoulders to get them through, then thrust his hands to either side for support.

It was not enough. Fargo felt himself slipping. He tried to catch hold of the bottom of the window but missed. The next thing he knew, he was tumbling onto wood Maria had piled close to the stove. His shoulder was jarred, but otherwise he was unhurt.

Rising, Fargo went around the stove, drawing up short in horror at the sight of a human leg protruding past the leg of a table across the kitchen. He dashed over.

Maria Caddo had been stabbed repeatedly. Someone had taken sadistic delight in making her suffer first. Her ears and nose had been cut off, her mouth was a bloody ruin. Not satisfied with mutilating her, the culprit had partially scalped her as well.

Revulsion and fury flooded through Fargo. Maria had been a timid, gentle soul, who in no way deserved the grisly death she had suffered. It would devastate Louis.

Louis! Pivoting, Fargo ran into the tavern so fast that he nearly tripped over an overturned chair. The place was a shambles. All the furniture had been upturned and pushed back against the walls and the bar, leaving a wide clear space in the middle of the floor. Sprawled there was the Cajun. He had been stripped to the waist and his shoes were gone.

Dreading what he would see, Fargo stepped closer. A lump of raw rage formed in his throat. Whole strips of skin had been flayed from Caddo's body. Deep cuts marred every square inch. The face was the worst. It had been slashed to ribbons. Glancing down, Fargo discovered that most of Louis's toes were missing, sliced off not by a knife or an ax or a tomahawk, but by a bullwhip. The marks it left could not be confused with anything else.

"Bullwhip Mulligan," Fargo said, the words lashing out like the whip itself. A burning sensation seared through him, and he clenched his fists, his arms quaking. In his wide-flung travels he had seen a lot of death. If pressed, he would admit that he had dispensed more than his fair share, too. But few had ever touched him as deeply as the murders of the Caddos. They had been friendly, decent people. They had not deserved their horrible ends.

What made it worse was knowing that, indirectly, Fargo was to blame. If he had never come into their lives, they would still *be* alive.

Fargo did not know how Bullwhip Mulligan had found out where the Caddos lived. Either Mulligan had recognized the Cajun and visited the tavern while Fargo was trying to find the redhead, or Mulligan had someone shadow Caddo from the domiciliary.

A light knock sounded on the front door.

Hand on the Colt, Fargo walked over and threw the bolt. He made a point of standing to one side as he cracked it open. For a second he thought that no one was there. Then he glanced down.

A barefoot boy of ten or so in tattered jeans and a thin shirt smiled up at him. "Hi. I'm Gerald. Is Mr. Caddo in? I have the news he wanted."

"You just missed him," Fargo lied. It was best to keep the deaths a secret until he collected his gear and got out of there. Past experience with the law had taught him that sometimes lawmen were a bit zealous when it came to solving a crime. They might detain him for hours, badgering him with questions.

"Darn," the boy said. "I had my heart set on some hard candy."

"Does he keep some here?" Fargo asked.

Gerald snickered. "You don't understand, mister. Mr. Caddo promised me a dollar. He asked me to keep watch down by the river and let him know when the *River Queen* got back from New Orleans." He paused. "Well, she got here about half an hour ago. She's moored down by the old wharf south of Fremont Street. Mr. Caddo will know where that is." Gerald began to go. "Tell him I'll be back for my money later, will you?"

"No. Wait." Fargo fished in a pocket, found a dollar, and handed it over. "This one is on me. Thanks for all your trouble."

"No bother at all," the boy said, admiring the coin. "Mr. Caddo has me run errands for him all the time. He's real nice. He always pays well." Beaming, Gerald skipped off to spend his newfound wealth.

Bolting the door, Fargo hurried to the cot at the rear. His bedroll was underneath, undisturbed. Wrapped in it was the Henry. He paused to glance one last time at Maria, then he went out the same way he had entered, through the window. Leaving both doors locked would prevent discovery of the bodies until at least that evening when the regulars arrived.

From the Brown Pelican Fargo went to the livery. His saddle was being held for safe keeping in the tack room. He slid his bedroll under it, left word with the owner to keep an eye on his rifle, and hastened down to the waterfront. The third person he asked knew where the *River Queen* was moored.

It was but one of half a dozen strung out along that section of the shore, a favorite berthing spot. But it was the grandest of the lot, being the widest and longest and sporting a fresh coat of bright white paint. Her twin stacks, over ninety feet high, shone in the sunlight. Passengers were still disembarking. Up a second gangplank freight was being loaded.

Fargo stood in the shadow of a building to study the riverboat from stem to stern. She had three decks, the bottom used to transport freight and to carry what were known as "deck passengers." They were people too poor to pay for private cabins, which were located on the middle deck along with a dining room and social hall, a gambling parlor, and others.

The third deck held a few lifeboats and the pilothouse or wheelhouse where the pilot and navigator spent all their time. It was raised well above the upper deck to give them an unobstructed view of the river both ahead of their vessel and to the rear.

Some deckhands were loading wood. The boilers that powered the paddles devoured it. Typically a steamboat would put into shore twice a day to wood up, as the chore was called.

Hooking his thumbs in his gun belt, Fargo strolled down to the water's edge and acted fascinated by the hustle and bustle. When one of the crewmen glanced at him, he remarked, "I hear tell that your boat makes regular runs to New Orleans. You don't happen to know when the next one is, do you?"

The man stopped to mop his brow. "Mister, we just got in. It'll be two days before we leave again. Some of us have families we like to see on occasion, you know."

Fargo turned to go, stopping when a small party appeared at the forward rail on the middle deck. Two were ravishing young women dressed in the finest of fashion. The third was a tall, imposing man Fargo had never laid eyes on before. But the other two men he knew, and they saw him at the same moment that he saw them.

Henri Lacombe gave a start, then smirked and waved. He said something to the tall man, who gazed intently at Fargo. Pritchard was also at the rail. The runt, as Torrance had called him, started to pull his pistol, but froze at a word from the tall one.

It had to be Jace De Cade. Clothed in the most expensive suit that money could buy, he reeked of power, of position. Four fingers bore rings inset with glittering gems. A thick gold watch chain adorned his vest. A diamond stickpin graced his narrow tie. His thick black hair was neatly cut, his mustache full and sweeping. In his left hand he held a cane crowned by an ivory eagle.

They locked eyes. Fargo swore he could feel De Cade's bore into him even at that distance. It was like the time he had been winding through the Rockies and looked up at a high ledge to find a mountain lion eyeing him. De Cade had the same intense presence about him.

Lacombe spoke. De Cade nodded. Instantly the Cajun and the runt sprinted toward the stairs that would bring them to the lower deck. Lacombe yelled and three other men fell into step behind them.

Fargo got out of there. He was not ready to lock horns with De Cade yet, not until Jasmine Tanner was safe and sound. Taking a side street, he put several blocks behind him. Quickly shimmying up a lamppost so he could see over the heads of the pedestrians, he confirmed the Cajun was still after him. Sliding down, he turned onto Broussard Street.

Not far off stood carriages for rent. Fargo climbed into the first one and slouched in the seat. When the driver bent to ask his destination, Fargo gave him the name of the livery. As the carriage rattled past the side street, Lacombe and the others appeared. They looked both ways but did not think to look into the carriage. Within seconds the flow of traffic hid them.

Fargo took stock of the situation and did not like the conclusions he reached. There could be no doubt now that De Cade was somehow linked to Jasmine's disappearance and those of the other bayou women. Whatever De Cade was up to was important enough for him to silence anyone who grew too curious by having them murdered.

Circumstances had pitted Fargo against one of the most powerful men in Baton Rouge, a man who had no scruples about killing and who could hire a legion of killers to get the job done. From then on he had to be on his toes every minute of the day and night. De Cade was not about to rest until he had been eliminated.

At the stable Fargo arranged to sleep in the hayloft later for a few extra dollars. The liveryman asked no questions, even providing an old blanket.

It was close to sunset when Fargo headed for the domiciliary. He came to the mouth of the same alley, only this time he walked down it from the other end in case lookouts had been posted at the hotel. Screened by shadows, he noted the comings and goings of the clientele. Women drifted in and out over the next hour and a half, sometimes singly, sometimes in pairs or small groups. Based on the number he saw, he calculated there must be thirty staying there.

An unusual fact soon became apparent. He had assumed that the women would be of all different ages, some young, some old, some in their middle years. But every last one appeared to be between eighteen and twenty-four. It couldn't be a coincidence. Yet the reason eluded him.

As if fate wanted to prove him right, an elderly woman wearing clothes that were on their last legs and toting a worn bag showed up. Her knock was answered by Mulligan. They were too far away for Fargo to hear what was said, but it was plain that she wanted to rent a room. Mulligan shook his head. The woman then talked at some length, as if she were pleading. She might as well have implored a rock. Bullwhip Mulligan rudely gestured for her to leave. When she was too slow to suit him, he pushed her.

The woman walked on down the street, her head hung low, her eyes moist.

Fargo saw a young woman approach. Mulligan, about to go back inside, smiled broadly and gave a little bow as he held the door for her. The bastard.

In due course the sun set. Darkness veiled Baton Rouge, broken by the rosy glow from windows and infrequent lamps. As yet Fargo had not seen any sign of the redhead.

Then the front door opened and out filed seven of the lovely maidens. They wore tight dresses, hats, and furs. One was the redhead who claimed to be Susan Clark. Oddly, for women about to go out on the town, not one was smiling or joking or laughing. By their expressions, a person would think they were on their way to a funeral.

With them were three men, Bullwhip Mulligan and two other toughs. The former raised an arm, beckoning. A trio of broughams that had been parked down the street rolled up. One man entered each, along with a couple of the ladies.

Fargo straightened. No carriages for hire were in sight. He was going to lose the redhead again. Edging forward, his right foot bumped something that made a tinkling noise as it rolled a few feet to the right. It was an empty bottle. Inspiration galvanized him into picking it up and hurling it at the hotel. He aimed for a second-floor window but the bottle smashed to bits above it, the crash of glass causing all eyes to focus on the building.

Bent low, Fargo bolted into the street, crossing in several long strides. The night hid him to some extent, while the rumble of an oncoming wagon drowned out what little noise he made. But he counted more on everyone being distracted for the precious seconds it took him to cross and duck under the first brougham.

Unlike the undercarriage of a covered wagon, there was no frame to hold onto. Nor were there footboards such as were found on most carriages. Broughams did have, however, circular metal steps suspended below the doors on both sides. Wrapping his arms around one, he hooked his ankles around the other. It was uncomfortable as could be.

Many of the women were talking all at once, wondering what had caused the noise. The cutthroat in the second brougham called out, "Bullwhip? Shouldn't we all get out and take a look?"

"No," Mulligan bellowed. "We might be late as it is, and you know how the boss gets when we are. It was probably those damn kids again. I swear. If I ever catch one, I'll strangle him!" He pounded on the back of the driver's seat. "Get going! And don't stop for anything."

The brougham gave a lurch. Fargo nearly lost his hold, but he held on as the vehicle veered into the middle of the street, gaining speed swiftly. He had to stay alert to keep from swaying too far to the right or the left. The front and rear wheels were dangerously close.

Muffled voices fell on his ears. The driver hummed softly. Drumming hooves nearly eclipsed both. Fargo bounced with every rut and hole they hit. When, moments later, they took a turn at high speed, he was hard pressed to keep from being hurled against the rear wheels.

It did not take long for Fargo's shoulders to ache terribly. His ankles grew sore. His wrists became chafed. Resigned to the pain, he held on with all his strength as the brougham negotiated a maze of streets. He had no idea where he was at any given point, but he did figure out where they were going before too long. The river.

The lead brougham swung into a side street as inky as the bottom of a well. Fargo could barely see his hands, let alone his feet. Suddenly the brougham hit a deep rut. Then another. And a third. Fargo clung tightly to the small steps, but his fingers started to slip anyway.

Bullwhip Mulligan cursed. "What the hell are you doing up there, Thompson? Making it a point to hit every hole there is?"

"You wanted to get there quickly," the driver replied. "I'm taking a shortcut."

The brougham struck the deepest rut yet. Fargo was flung against the bottom of the vehicle, then swung toward the rear. A wheel gouged into his shoulder. For a few harrowing seconds, he thought that he would be torn from his perch. He managed to hold on and craned his neck to see how close they were to the Mississippi.

A gaping dark spot materialized ahead. "Brace yourselves!" the driver shouted.

Fargo had nothing to brace himself against. The right side plowed into the hole and was catapulted a foot or higher into the air. Fargo's ankles lost their grip. His legs sagged and were dragged, the friction hurting almost as much as the strain on his shoulders. He had to let go or be torn off. Rolling as he dropped, he knifed his legs straight so the wheels would miss them.

The brougham passed over him. Fargo had saved himself from serious injury, but he was not safe. The second brougham bore down rapidly, its team unable to distinguish his form in the gloom. Their heavy hooves hammered nearer and nearer as he coiled to fling himself out of harm's way. His right hand, scrambling for purchase, plunged into a hole instead, dumping him on his chest.

The horses were almost on top of him.

10

It took big, sturdy horses to pull broughams. Introduced in England, they were larger and heavier than typical carriages and coupes.

The pair of animals that loomed over Skye Fargo seemed like gargantuan beasts from a bygone age. He saw their nostrils flare, heard the wheeze of their breathing an instant before he hurled himself to the right. Stones scraped his palms. His shoulder was lanced by a brief pang. Then the ground fell out from under him, and he rolled down an incline into tall grass. A sharp object tore at his leg but did no serious damage. He grabbed his hat when it began to slide off.

Propped on his elbows, Fargo saw the second brougham recede into the night. The third went by moments later, the driver clucking to the horses. Framed in a window was the lovely face of Susan Clark. She was gazing wistfully into the distance.

Fargo stood and stiffly climbed out. No other vehicles were coming. No one had seen his narrow escape. The element of surprise still worked in his favor. Slapping his holster to see if he still had the Colt, he followed the broughams, the retreating clatter of their wheels guiding him to their destination only a few hundred yards away.

The *River Queen* was ablaze with light. Music jingled on the night air. A steady murmur of voices floated toward the stars. People thronged the three decks. At first Fargo thought the crewman had been wrong earlier and the steamboat was preparing to depart. As he drew nearer, he discovered that all those on board were dressed in elegant fashion, many holding drinks. They strolled along the rails or talked and joked.

Jace De Cade was throwing a social affair. The cream of Baton Rouge society was there, all those who lived in the big mansions that overlooked the river, those who like De Cade had money to spare. Gold jewelry flashed on every hand and every female throat. Silk and satin and Prince Albert coats were the order of the day. It had to be one of the premier events of the year and would be royally written up in the newspaper the next day.

Carriages, cabriolets, phaetons, surreys, and other vehicles crammed the shore. The three broughams pulled up next to the gangplank to unload their passengers, then moved on to find a spot to park.

Bullwhip Mulligan swaggered up the gangplank as if he owned the boat. He said a few words to two burly men who stood at the top before ushering the women into the crowd.

Fargo came to the shore and moved to the left, among the vehicles. Some of the drivers had not climbed down and were smoking or resting. Others had gathered in knots to pass the time. He avoided them all.

The two crewmen standing guard at the gangplank were not about to let him on board. He had to find another way. Accordingly, stealthily moving to the water's edge, he was on the verge of wading in and swimming when a nearby mound of driftwood gave him a better idea.

Poking among the pile, Fargo found several sizable logs. One was light enough to pry from the tangle and push into the river where it bobbed gently. Straddling it, he moved into deeper water. When his feet could no longer touch bottom, he laid on his belly and paddled, stroking out onto the broad Mississippi. He was far enough downriver that the light from the steamboat would not reveal him to watchful eyes.

Fargo made for the stern, three hundred and fifty feet

out. The log was so buoyant that he barely got wet. It cleaved the surface nicely and all went well until he was two dozen yards from land. A sudden push by an invisible hand was all the warning Fargo had that the current was much stronger than he had reckoned on. He paddled harder to compensate, and for a while he sailed smoothly.

The farther he went, though, the worse the current became. Presently he was fighting for every yard he gained. After a while his arms grew heavy. The log began to drift. Redoubling his effort, he managed another thirty feet. Then, for some reason he could not fathom, the current stopped buffeting him. He took advantage of the lull and quickly closed the gap, coming around on the stern.

Fewer people were aft than forward. There were less lanterns and consequently much less light. Here and there couples clung to one another or whispered in intimate conversation. No guards were in evidence, but Fargo took no chances. Gliding soundlessly in close enough to prop his hands against the side, he steadied the log and rose into a crouch.

Steamboat drafts were shallow. They had to be to permit the vessels to range as far up the Mississippi as they did. The average was two to six feet. On some boats the lower deck was so close to the water that passengers could dip their hands in as they cruised along.

In the *River Queen*'s case, the deck rose only three and a half feet above the surface. It was simple for Fargo to straighten, grip the edge, and pull himself onto the steamboat. The spot he had picked was one of the darkest. He had not seen anyone near it, so he was startled when someone cooed softly. Lying still, barely breathing, he saw a man and woman over by a bunch of crates. The woman's dress was up around her hips, and the man was stroking her. Neither had any interest in the world around them. They never noticed when Fargo rose and glided to where bales formed a square stack.

Making it on board had been just the first step. Now Fargo had to find the redhead, and that promised to be a challenge. Dressed as he was, he would stand out in the well-to-do crowd. As he stood there pondering, a loud kiss caught his attention.

Off to the left was another couple. As he looked on, the woman knelt and tugged at the man's pants.

Over by the north rail, yet another pair were in a passionate embrace, the man groping the woman under her clothes, the woman panting heavily. They were nearer to a lantern than anyone else, and Fargo was surprised to see that it was one of the young women who lived at the domiciliary.

He moved forward. Thanks to the freight loaded that day, there were plenty of hiding places. He saw more couples locked together, so many that he began to wonder what was going on. A few would be understandable, but dozens? It was almost as if the aft portion of the riverboat had been purposely left dark just so romantic pairs could indulge themselves. But that seemed out of keeping with the reputation De Cade had of being an upper-crust businessman.

Crouched behind a row of barrels, Fargo stared at the stairs leading up to the middle deck. Above milled Baton Rouge's high society. Mixing with them were men in long white coats, waiters carrying silver trays laden with drinks and snacks. One of them came toward the steps and descended, an empty tray in hand. Turning, he opened a door and vanished. On reappearing minutes later, he carried a freshly filled tray.

Fargo smiled. Bearing to the left, he hurried to a corner close to the door. No other waiters were anywhere in sight. Nor were any lovemakers. A buckskin streak, he entered and immediately stepped down a narrow hall that led to a spacious kitchen where pots clanged and men were yelling back and forth. None of the staff noticed him. Ducking into an open doorway, Fargo found himself in a supply room. In addition to the goods lining the shelves, several spare white coats hung on hooks on the right wall.

He selected the largest. It was the only one that would fit over his buckskins, and it was a tight fit, at that. From the knees up he would pass for a waiter. Unfortunately, he could not wear his hat. It would be a dead giveaway. He might as well tote a sign saying, *Mulligan and Lacombe, here I am*! Taking it off, he gently pressed it in upon itself and tucked it under his shirt over his stomach. The effect was to give him a noticeable paunch, which helped with his disguise.

Inching the door open, he checked the hall, then hurried to the outer door and onto the deck. A portly waiter was coming down the stairs carrying an empty tray. His brow was dotted with perspiration, and he walked stiffly.

"Are you all right?" Fargo asked.

The man licked thick lips and shook his head. "I told that damn Howard I was sick, but would he believe me? No! I think I'm coming down with the flu."

"Want me to take that tray for you? I'm not doing anything else at the moment."

The man looked as if he would burst into tears. "Would you? I'd be so grateful. I need to sit down for a while and rest, or I'm liable to keel over. I'm so hot, I'm roasting."

"I'd be glad to help," Fargo said, accepting the tray. He pointed aft. "If you want some peace and quiet, I'd try back there."

"Thanks, friend."

As the man walked off, Fargo twirled the tray, chuckled, and headed for the middle deck. He blended into the crowd, moving about as if he knew just where he was going, all the while searching for that distinctive red mane. He glimpsed reddish hair and turned, thinking he had found her at last. But it was an older woman wearing a mink cape lined at the collar with red fox fur.

A complete circuit of the open area failed to turn up Clark. Fargo was about to climb the companionway to the upper deck when he thought to check the cabins and the dining hall. Walking aft along a wide passageway, he spied a bald pate ahead. Halting at a cabin door, he knocked. When there was no answer, he tried the latch. The door was unlocked, the cabin empty. He darted into it just in time. Moments later, Bullwhip Mulligan strutted by with two cutthroats in tow.

Fargo resumed his search. It occurred to him that the red-head might be in any of the cabins. But there were dozens. He would check them only as a last resort.

The wide doors to the dining hall had been propped open. It was a magnificent saloon, over two hundred feet long, lit by crystal chandeliers that hung from beams bordering stained-glass skylights. An overflow crowd filled every seat, ringed every table, packed the open space except in the middle where couples danced gaily. On a raised platform the orchestra played. Fargo mingled among the throng, ignoring anyone who called out for him to fetch a drink.

There were so many people that finding Susan Clark seemed a hopeless task. Fargo scoured every nook, examined every face. He was two thirds of the way across the hall when he saw a particular table that had been set slightly apart from the rest. At its head sat none other than Jace De Cade. Seven other well-dressed men and eight beautiful women shared the table of honor with him.

Of more importance to Fargo was one of the women near the opposite end. He had found Susan Clark at last. She was seated next to an older gentleman—if that was what he could be called—who leaned on her shoulder and openly pawed her. Yet she did not lift a finger to hinder him.

Some of the other women were familiar, too. He had seen them go into or leave the domiciliary at one time or another. All were paired with older men. Most, like the red-head, acted resigned to their fate.

Fargo moved over against the left wall, where he was out

of the way of everyone else. Holding the tray so that it partially screened his face, he edged close enough to overhear what Jace De Cade was saying. The man had a deep baritone voice, in keeping with his commanding presence.

"Senator Blackmun, Congressman Sneed, and my other distinguished guests. I propose that we drink a toast." De Cade raised his long-stemmed glass, and the others followed suit. "To our mutual prosperity, my friends. May there be no end to it."

"Amen to that," declared the man at the redhead's side. Swallowing greedily, he smacked his thin lips, then leered at Clark. "I must say, Jace, that you have knack for finding the most exquisite creatures."

"I spare no expense, Senator," De Cade said. "It's a token of the esteem in which I hold all of you. For I know that if the need arose, you would not hesitate to be of as much help to me as I have been to you."

The senator gulped more champagne. "You can count on me," he stated, dribbling over his lower lip. "If not for you, I would have lost the last campaign. How you managed to get the vote to turn out the way it did, I'll never know."

De Cade smiled. "We all have our little secrets, Senator. Suffice it to say that there are ways of persuading people to cast their ballots for the right person even if they are not so inclined."

Titters spread around the table, but only the men and one or two women joined in. Susan Clark was not one of them. Extending her empty glass for a hovering waiter to fill, she drank with no enthusiasm. It caught the attention of their host.

"Is something the matter, my dear Miss Clark?"

The redhead stiffened in transparent fright. She quickly recovered her composure and said, "Not at all, Mr. De Cade. I'm enjoyin' myself immensely."

"Then, perhaps you should *act* like you are," De Cade informed her, flint in every syllable. "After all, how can you expect our esteemed guests to have a good time if you are not? Wasn't it made clear to you how crucial your role is? If not, I'm more than willing to take you to my private quarters and personally instruct you."

Fargo knew a veiled threat when he heard one. He saw Clark blanch, but the woman had spunk. She meet De Cade's fiery gaze and responded, "Don't fret yourself, sir. I know what is required of me. I would never let you down."

De Cade's smile grew as brittle as old china. "See that you don't, lovely one. The consequences are not to be taken lightly, I assure you."

Senator Blackmun slapped his glass down and rose unsteadily. "Enough flapping our gums! I'm in need of some fresh air, and I'd be delighted if this beautiful young lady would accompany me." Lifting the redhead's hand, he kissed her knuckles. "Would you, sweet thing?"

It was Jace De Cade who answered for her. "Of course she will, Senator. And if she gives you any argument, any at all, please feel free to inform me right away. There are many other young lovelies who would be honored to have your undivided attention."

The senator snickered and pulled back Clark's chair so she could stand. She smiled demurely, but anyone who was not half drunk could have told that she would rather slit her throat than go along. De Cade studied her as they left, and he was scowling.

Fargo was glad to get out of there. It was only a matter of time before one of De Cade's men caught on to him. He hugged the wall, keeping track of the politician and the redhead as they threaded through the throng to the double doors. They bore to the right and so did he. Blackmun was leaning on her again, his free hand roaming where it willed.

Staying in the shadows, Fargo trailed them to a junction. The senator steered Clark to the left. She balked, digging in her heels and saying, "Where are you takin' me, sir? I thought we were going aft."

Blackmun playfully tugged on her wrist. "No, no, no. I've been to these affairs before, dearie. We wouldn't have the privacy I desire back there. So we're going to my cabin, if it's all right with you." He unexpectedly twisted her wrist, making her grimace. "And even if it isn't all right. You heard your lord and master. Do as I say or he'll make you suffer in ways you can not imagine."

Susan Clark clenched her fists but did not take a poke at the senator. Her shoulders slumped in defeat, and she was hauled toward a cabin door where Blackmun paused to fish in a pocket for his key.

"Now, where the devil is it? I know I put—" The senator chortled and yanked it out. Swaying, he had to try twice before he could insert the key, then he had to jiggle it to get the door open. "After you, my dear"—shoving her through ahead of him.

Fargo was a step behind as the politician entered. Neither Blackmun nor Clark were aware of him until the senator went to close the door and his body blocked the opening. "Excuse me, Senator," he said.

"What the hell?" Blackmun blurted, turning. "Who asked you in here? What do you want?"

"Just this," Fargo said, and brought the silver tray down on the crown of the crooked politico's head with all his might. The tray buckled and so did Blackmun, sinking to the carpet without another word. Fargo promptly closed the door and faced the redhead.

"You!"

"Hello again, Jasmine Tanner."

She took a step back, a palm over her mouth. Her features rippled, mirroring a bitter conflict waged in the depths of her soul. A low groan escaped her lips. Weaving as if dizzy, she staggered to the bed and sat. "Who are you?" she asked weakly. "Why do you keep showing up?"

"Jessie sent me, Jasmine. Your mother and sister are worried to death. They want you to come home."

Tears poured from her eyes. She tried to stifle them, but it was like trying to plug a break in a damn. She cried and cried, finding a release that must have been long denied. After the longest time the tears trickled to low sobs. Dabbing her eyes, she said, "I'm sorry. I don't know what came over me." She gestured. "You must go before they find you. I don't want your death on my conscience."

"You're coming with me," Fargo said.

She shook her head. "I wish I could. Just go back and tell my mother and sister that you couldn't find me, and let it go at that. It's better all around if they never see me again."

"I can't do that." Fargo took her hand in his and squeezed gently. "I gave your sister my word that I would bring you back safe and sound, and that's what I aim to do."

A loud voice outside caused Jasmine to jump. Glancing fearfully at the small window, she said, "Listen to me, mister. You don't know what you are up against here. I can't leave, whether I want to or not."

"Why?" Fargo probed. "Why did you change your name to Susan Clark? Why are you staying at that hotel? Why let De Cade walk all over you?"

Jasmine Tanner was a study in misery. "If only I could tell you," she said wistfully. "Let's just say I made a mistake and let it go at that. Now, *you* go." She pushed him toward the door. "Please. For both our sakes."

"No." Fargo bluntly refused, and stressed, "I'm not leaving without you." Her attitude was baffling. He had thought she would be overjoyed at the prospect of being reunited with her family. "You can't want to stay. Not with how they treat you."

More tears flowed. "If you only knew," she sighed.

Every second they delayed chafed Fargo's nerves. His gut instinct was to get off the *River Queen* right away. Senator Blackmun was bound to revive soon and would squawk to high heaven unless they gagged him. Or someone might stop by to pay their respects. "There's not time to argue," he said. "If you want to see Jessie and your mom again, come with me right this minute."

Jasmine rose uncertainly, wiping her eyes on the sleeve of her dress. "It will never work. They won't let you take me."

"Let me worry about De Cade and his men." Stripping off the white jacket, Fargo replaced it with the senator's Prince Albert coat. His hat under his left arm, he held Jasmine's hand and stepped to the door. The passageway was empty. "Stay close no matter what happens," he said.

The companionway to the lower deck was forward. Fargo hustled the redhead to a corner. Beyond was the rail and the stairs. Guests packed the deck, few giving Fargo a second glance as he navigated through them, Jasmine right beside him, the soft contours of her body glued to his. Despite their plight, Fargo felt a stirring below his belt.

As they reached the top step, a pair of crewmen started up from below. Fargo squared his shoulders and kept on going, ready to draw if the pair confronted them. But they walked on by, talking about a vessel that had wrecked on a submerged snag the year before.

Jasmine's nails dug into Fargo's arm, and she pressed even closer. He clasped her hand more firmly to reassure her, but she was too upset to be soothed. "We'll never make it," she breathed. "Please go on without me. I don't want you hurt."

"We'll be fine," Fargo said, but even he had to admit that they would be bucking the odds if he got her off without a hitch. At the bottom he headed straight for the gangplank, or as straight as he could with the deck jammed by the city's upper crust.

The same two cutthroats stood guard. One was lighting a cigarette. The other was gazing across the river. Neither made a move to stop them.

Fargo had done it! "See?" he told Jasmine, the gangplank bouncing a little with every step they took. Drivers clustered nearby paid no attention to them as they angled through the parked vehicles toward the nearest street. "We'll collect your things," he said, "and in a few days you'll be safe in your cabin."

"I'll never be safe," Jasmine responded, "not so long as Lacombe is alive."

Behind a carriage on the right, someone laughed. "Ain't it the truth, though, *chéri*?" Into the open strode the hawk-faced Cajun, and he was not alone. Bullwhip Mulligan flanked him on one side, Pritchard on the other. Three other men stepped from concealment, spreading out as they did.

"Oh, God!" Jasmine said.

Bullwhip Mulligan had his coiled whip in hand. Shaking it at Fargo, he rasped, "I was hopin' I'd get another crack at you, mister. Say your prayers."

With that, the bullwhip lashed out.

11

Skye Fargo gave Jasmine Tanner a shove and shouted, "Run for it!" as the tip of the whip bit into his shoulder. She darted off but was caught by Henri Lacombe, who savagely twisted her left arm behind her back.

"Where are you going, *ma petite?* We wouldn't want you to miss all the fun, eh? Stay and see what happens to those who defy the big man."

Bullwhip Mulligan circled to the right, his whole squat frame as tense as a wolverine about to pounce. "Where should I start, Lacombe? With his eyes? Or maybe his nose, like I did with Louis Caddo?"

Fargo was trapped, surrounded by his enemies, unable to go for his pistol without being gunned down by Pritchard and the three hardcases who had him covered. He tried to keep as much distance as he could between Mulligan and himself so he would have time to react to the next swing. It was a futile notion.

The bulldog's arm barely moved, and the bullwhip snaked up off the ground, sizzling the air as it shot toward Fargo more swiftly than the human eye could follow. He dodged to one side, but the whip caught him anyway, across the thigh. The pain was excruciating.

Mulligan sneered as Fargo hobbled a few yards. "Hurt, did it? I've got news for you. It's just the beginning."

With a sustained hiss, the bullwhip leaped forward again. And again. And again. Fargo ducked, danced aside, weaved, and bobbed. He was hit repeatedly, but by keeping in motion he prevented the lash from inflicting severe wounds. He stung. He hurt. Once a two-inch gash in his shin was opened. But he stayed on his feet and continued to circle until he was directly across from Henri Lacombe and the redhead.

For a moment Fargo paused and glanced at Jasmine. He did not relish what he had to do next. In her eyes it might brand him as a coward. Yet it was their only hope. To save her, he had to survive. To survive, he had to abandon her, if only for a short while.

Bullwhip Mulligan had grown cockier. Chuckling with sadistic mirth, he feinted a few times, flicking the whip but not connecting. Abruptly he swung in earnest, moving in closer when Fargo skipped backward.

It never occurred to the bald cutthroat that Fargo had a reason for darting straight back other than the obvious one of eluding the whip. For while circling, Fargo had positioned himself in front of the three gunmen. When he flew backward, he flew toward them. He was banking on the trio doing one of two things. Either they would grab hold of him and shove him toward Mulligan, or they would scatter to get out of the way of Mulligan's crackling whip. They picked the latter. The instant they did, Fargo whirled and dived under a carriage.

Lusty oaths were flung at him. Lacombe bawled, *"Mon Dieu!* You stupid clods! After him! If he gets away, the boss will have our heads!"

Clear of the undercarriage, Fargo rose and ran around the rear of a phaeton, a large open vehicle with a canopy top. The Colt leaped from its scabbard. Spinning, he glimpsed two shapes rushing past the carriage. A pistol boomed, and he answered in kind, twice. One of the figures pitched over, the other made himself scarce.

"Get him!" Lacombe screeched. "Damn it all, *don't let him escape!"*

Fargo ran on. The gunshots had drawn loud shouts from the drivers. The smart ones sought cover. Those with more curiosity than brains were rushing over to find out what all the shooting was about. From the steamboat came questioning yells.

A prancing team gave Fargo an idea. Bellowing like a riled grizzly, he fired into the ground beside the horses, and they predictably bolted. Since they were hemmed in by other vehicles, they had nowhere to go and wound up pushing against other vehicles in front of them. Their panic became contagious. Other horses whinnied and pranced. Unattended carriages and coupés and whatnot moved every which way as the frightened animals tried to flee. Soon the shore was sheer bedlam, with angry drivers striving to bring their teams under control.

In all the confusion, no one paid any attention to Fargo as he wound southward. He could still hear Lacombe bawling when he passed the last of the vehicles. By rights he should be thrilled that he had saved himself, but all he could think of was Jasmine. He turned to scan the area where he had left her. As he did, a short, lithe form shot from under the nearest carriage and slammed into his legs, bowling him over. Steel flashed at his shoulder. Only because he had fallen with his arm on his chest was he able to block the blow.

Pritchard growled like a ferret and swung his long knife again, seeking to cripple rather than kill. This time the blade wanged off the Colt, jarring the revolver from Fargo's grasp. Fargo landed a cross to the jaw that knocked the smaller man off him. Surging upright, he drew the toothpick as he stood.

"Thought you gave us the slip, did you?" Pritchard crowed, holding his long knife low, the keen edge out, just as any skilled knife fighter would do. "Think again."

Fargo parried a thrust aimed at his ribs. Until that moment Pritchard had not realized he had a knife of his own. The clang of ringing metal made the small man jump clear and regard Fargo warily.

"So. A blade man, too. Let's see how good you are."

Pritchard waded in again, his knife weaving an intricate pattern that would have sliced through the guard of most foes. Fargo was hard-pressed to hold his own. He shut all conscious thought from his mind and reacted on pure reflex, countering swing after swing and striking when he saw openings.

Back in the bayou, Pritchard had bragged about his skill with a blade. He had not exaggerated. Fargo had met few who could rival the short firebrand. If the fight were to go on indefinitely, Pritchard would win.

But skill was not the only deciding factor in battle. The weapons used could also make a difference.

The small man's knife was half as long as his arm, a wicked instrument designed for cutting and carving. Fargo's Arkansas toothpick, however, was smaller and slimmer and designed to be thrown, as well as for close-in fighting. So throw it Fargo did, just when Pritchard stepped back from his vicious onslaught. In a smooth underhand toss, Fargo sank the toothpick into the feisty killer's chest.

Pritchard jerked as if slapped, then looked down at himself and gave a gurgling laugh. "I'll be damned," he said softly. "That's a new one on me." Grinning crookedly, he toppled forward, landing on the toothpick and driving it deeper into his body.

Fargo located the Colt. Nudging Pritchard with a toe, he verified the killer was dead before he rolled the body over. He had to tug and tear to free the toothpick. The blade he wiped clean on Pritchard's shirt. As he stood, Bullwhip Mulligan called out from somewhere north of him.

"Pritchard? Did you get the saddle tramp?"

"No, he didn't!" Fargo answered, and he did the very last thing his enemies would expect. He went back in among the vehicles, crabbing along in a crouch, keeping the steamboat in sight as much as he could. The babble of voices made it clear that De Cade's sterling social event had been thoroughly disrupted.

All three decks were jammed with onlookers. Near the gangplank a dozen of De Cade's men had congregated, many with rifles. Fargo hunkered behind a surrey and saw the big man himself shoulder through the throng to the edge of the lower deck.

Jace De Cade faced his guests and raised both arms to instill quiet. "Please, ladies and gentlemen!" he said. "There is no cause for alarm! Whatever has happened, my people can deal with it. Go on enjoying yourselves. There is plenty of champagne left and food for anyone who is hungry."

Some of the guests started to turn. They froze when a crewman walked out from among the vehicles dragging the limp body of the man Fargo had shot. Lacombe and Jasmine were a few paces behind, the Cajun no longer twisting her arm but walking so close to her that he might as well have been her own shadow.

An elderly woman on the upper deck cried out. Everyone commenced jabbering at once, and there was a concerted rush toward the gangplank by many on the lower deck. De Cade tried to stem the tide by insisting that all was well, but he could barely be heard above the riot of voices. Bullwhip Mulligan appeared, rushing to his boss and saying something in De Cade's ear. De Cade surveyed the vehicles, his face a mask of livid wrath. He bestowed the same look on Jasmine, and she cringed.

Fargo tread nearer. Only about a third of the guests were leaving. The rest were content to go on with the festivities. To show them the error of their ways, he emptied the Colt into the air. It provoked many of the teams into another panic and did likewise with the people still on board. Some flattened, as if they thought the shots had been fired at them. In short order a mass exodus was underway.

Strangely Jace De Cade made no attempt to stop them this time.

Fargo had no trouble slipping unnoticed from among the vehicles to the mound of driftwood at the water's edge. He saw De Cade bark orders and eight or nine cutthroats fan out into the milling conveyances to hunt him down. A coupé was the first to leave, rattling up the grade into the city. Soon others streamed inland. The men hunting Fargo were at risk of being trampled by some of the panic-stricken guests.

Ten minutes later, only a handful of carriages were left. De Cade gestured at the Cajun and Jasmine. Lacombe prodded her up the gangplank, cuffing her when she stumbled.

Almost all the guests were gone. The few who remained made for the middle deck and the saloon. About that time one of De Cade's men found Pritchard. At a command from De Cade all the river men went back on board with the body. Last of all to climb the gangplank was De Cade himself. He twisted at the top to glare into the night, then he moved aft with most of his underlings. Three stayed behind.

It aggravated Fargo to think that after all he had just been through, he was no closer to rescuing the redhead than he had been when he got there. While most of the bystanders were out of harm's way, there was still a small army of killers to contend with.

Fargo pondered his choices. It came down to one. Since sneaking onto the *River Queen* and spiriting Jasmine to safety had not worked, it was time to try a more direct approach. Every minute he delayed might be a minute less Jasmine had to live. De Cade was bound to punish her, or worse.

He stripped off the Prince Albert coat, slapped his hat into shape, and placed it on his head. Reloading his Colt, he took a deep breath, then rose and walked toward the river-boat. The three guards saw him when he was forty feet out, but they did not bring their rifles to bear. Why should they? Only the crewmen who had been with Lacombe and Mulligan could recognize him on sight, and one of them was dead. None of the other river men knew him from Adam. To the guards he was just someone taking a late-night stroll along the river.

"Howdy," Fargo said, adopting a Texas twang and pushing his hat back. "I heard shots up this way awhile ago. What was all the ruckus about?"

The tallest man sneered. "Take a hike, cowboy. We're not paid to stand around and jaw with every busybody who passes by."

"Why don't you boys take the hike?" Fargo retorted, drawing and training his pistol on the spokesman. "Set down those rifles nice and slow unless you want windows in your skulls."

They glanced at one another. The burning question they had to answer was whether they could drop him before he dropped them. They had him outnumbered and would probably come out on top, but one or two of them were bound to take slugs.

"Now," Fargo stressed, raking the middle and upper decks for crewmen who might spread an alarm. So far fate was smiling on him.

"Our boss will kill us if we do," said one of the men.

"I'll kill you if you don't," Fargo replied. "I guess it boils down to how much longer you want to live."

The tall river man's nerve broke first. Holding the Spencer by the barrel, he lowered it. His example spurred the other two into doing the same.

Fargo hefted the Colt. "Step on down here." He backed up so they could not jump him as they filed onto shore. None were wearing revolvers that he could see. "Head into Baton Rouge and don't look back. If you do, you had better be able to dodge bullets."

The veiled threat worked. They marched swiftly off. Then, as they came to the street, the tall one made a comment to the others and all three laughed.

What was that about? Fargo wondered as he went up the gangplank. The lower deck was deserted. He rushed to the companionway and took the steps three at a time. No guests lined the middle deck, either. From the social hall drifted the melodious harmony of a waltz being played.

It unsettled Fargo that no other crewmen were evident. Where had they gotten to? Gliding down the passageway that went by Senator Blackmun's room, he tried the door. No one was inside. Even the bent tray was gone.

Given the *River Queen*'s size, it would take Fargo the better part of an hour to cover every square foot. Jasmine might not have that long. He jogged to the junction, pausing to glance to the right and the left. No one was in sight. Acting on the hunch that De Cade and company were in the saloon, he sprinted to the double doors.

They were closed. Fargo leaned against one and shouldered it open wide enough for him to scour the extravagant chamber. The orchestra played on. Those couples who had remained were either dancing or drinking. Of De Cade and Lacombe there was not a trace.

Fargo eased the door shut. He had not checked the upper deck yet so he did so now, jogging to the companionway amidships. The top deck was mainly a vast promenade where passengers could stroll at their leisure. The only structures were the wheelhouse and the texas, which was another name for the captain's quarters. In front of them towered the smokestacks. Forward, near the rail, were twin spars used to propel the boat over sandbars.

No lanterns pierced the gloom. The wheelhouse and texas were both dark. Fargo moved aft. On either side reared the housings for the massive paddle wheels. He suddenly halted on spying a hunched-over figure between them. No light was needed to make out the spilled mane of hair and the tight dress. Jasmine was on her knees, her arms bound behind her, her shoulders quaking.

She was bait, plain and simple.

Fargo did not try to run off while he could. He did not seek to hide. He simply holstered the Colt and walked over to the redhead. At his touch she gasped and recoiled, tears glistening on her cheeks. "It's me," he said, "and I won't be leaving you again."

"No!" Jasmine exclaimed. "They were hopin' you'd show! Get out of here before it's too late!"

From out of the shadow of the pilothouse slunk the lurkers who had been waiting for him. Henri Lacombe laughed and said, "It's already too late, *chérie*. Your knight in shining armor is about to have his head handed to him on this." He tossed the crumpled silver tray that Fargo had used to knock out the senator. It clattered noisily, tumbling to rest almost at Fargo's feet.

Bullwhip Mulligan was another of the eight men who cautiously spread out in a widening circle. Cracking his whip on the deck, he said, "Twice now you've gotten away from me, mister. It won't happen a third time."

Fargo helped Jasmine to stand. In her ear he whispered, "Be ready when I make my move."

The crewmen formed a ring, rifles leveled. Lacombe had shifted to the left, Mulligan to the right. Into the gap between them ambled their employer. Jace De Cade twirled his cane, then rested the tip on his shoulder and regarded Fargo and the redhead smugly. "I knew you would return for her," he said. "Bullwhip figured we would never see you again. But a man like you doesn't run off and desert someone in need. That's why I arranged this little reception."

Fargo had the feeling De Cade expected him to be flattered. Far from it. "I'm surprised you didn't have me shot from ambush. That's what a snake in the grass usually does."

De Cade pursed his lips. "I considered it, I'll confess. But I realized that it would not do to have you slain outright. There are questions I need answered." He stepped a few feet nearer. "We'll start with the most obvious. Who are you?"

"It's not important," Fargo said, casually turning so his right foot was next to the tray.

"I beg to differ," De Cade said. "You're not just a bumbling backwoodsman come to rescue his maiden fair. You're an outsider. An enigma. And I hate enigmas."

"What are those, boss?" Bullwhip Mulligan interjected. "Is he some kind of danged foreigner?"

De Cade rolled his eyes skyward. "An enigma, Mr. Mulligan, is beyond your feeble comprehension. Suffice it to say that we must learn all we can about our mystery man here."

Henri Lacombe shrugged. "Why bother, eh? Let me slit his throat and be done with it. We'll dump his carcass in the river on our way to New Orleans, and no one will ever be the wiser."

"Incompetents," Jace De Cade muttered. "I'm surrounded by incompetents." He stepped closer to Fargo and jabbed the cane at him. "Where did this man come from? Why did he show up the same week as my grand gathering, when I was about to clinch an important deal? Is he working alone or for someone else? Is he, perhaps, working for the federal government?" De Cade rounded on Lacombe. "Do you have the answers, Henri?"

"Non, monsieur."

"What about you, Bullwhip?"

Mulligan fidgeted. "You know I don't boss. But don't you worry. I can make this guy tell us whatever you want him to." He cracked his whip once more to punctuate his point.

Gesturing into the air, De Cade said to Fargo, "Is it any wonder you were able to get the better of them?" Sighing, he paced a few steps back and forth. "I don't suppose you would care to make this easy on both of us and put my mind at rest? The alternative will be most painful."

"First you tell me something," Fargo said. Nodding at

Jasmine, he asked, "How does she and all those other women fit into your scheme?"

De Cade was amused. "You haven't guessed yet? I'm surprised." He swept the steamboat from bow to stern with his cane. "As you no doubt have noticed, I like the very best life has to offer. Such elegance does not come cheaply. I've had to toil and sweat to make my riches."

While De Cade elaborated, Fargo noted the position of each and every crewman. His right toe slid a fraction closer to the crumpled tray.

"Funny thing, though. The wealthier I became, the more wealth I wanted. Like a child with a sweet tooth, I could never get enough. I became the richest man in Baton Rouge, then richer than anyone in New Orleans, and now I'm working on becoming the wealthiest in the entire state. Why, a few more years, and I'll have more money than John Jacob Astor himself."

Fargo knew who Astor was. The New Yorker had made a vast personal fortune in the fur trade and at the time of his death had been widely regarded as the richest person in America. None of which interested him in the least. "Why the women?" he repeated.

De Cade rested his cane on the deck and leaned on it. "I'm getting to that." He pointed at the tray. "You might not know it, but the man whose head you decorated with that is an important politician. I've found that to expand my business empire, I must court him and men like him. That means I must provide them with fine dinners and finer women on occasion."

In a flash of insight, Skye Fargo understood everything. "You force the women to sell their bodies," he said in disgust. "Lacombe acts as your pimp and brings you all the pretty young ones you need—"

The Cajun bristled. Taking a step, he clenched a fist. "Mark my words, *mon ami*. You will pay dearly for that insult. I guarantee."

De Cade held up a hand. "Pimp is such an indelicate word. I prefer to think of Mr. Lacombe as my procurement agent. Yes, he roams from one end of the bayou to the other in search of the loveliest flowers for my collection."

"You filth!" Jasmine practically screamed, and went to hurl herself at De Cade. Fargo caught her before she could take a step. "Tell him the rest! Tell him how Lacombe forces us to come whether we want to or not! Tell him how you threaten to kill our families if we won't go to bed with whoever you pick!"

"Please, my dear," De Cade chided. "Lower your voice. We're all adults here. This display is most unseemly."

"Unseemly?" Jasmine roared, and tried to kick him even though he was six feet away. "After what you've done to me, I want to rip your heart out with my bare hands! You're a monster!"

"Am I indeed?" Jace De Cade said, then laughed. So did Lacombe. Bullwhip Mulligan looked from one to the other, confused. That tickled the funny bone of several crewmen.

Fargo could not have planned it better if he tried. Hardly any of them were staring at him. They had even neglected to confiscate the Colt. Pressing his lips to Jasmine's ear, he whispered, "Now!" and exploded into action.

12

Skye Fargo had to wonder how Jace De Cade had climbed so high and lasted so long making as many mistakes as he did. The man was so sure of himself that he was outright careless. In the wilds of the Rockies or the fierce heart of the plains, De Cade would not last a week.

Now, with De Cade laughing merrily at Jasmine's expense, Fargo kicked the silver tray to one side. It clattered across the deck, drawing the gaze of every gunman. At the same instant, Fargo flew toward the wheelhouse. One hand gripped Jasmine, the other cleared the Colt. He banged a shot at a crewman who raised a rifle, another at the Cajun, who dived and rolled.

"Get them!" Bullwhip Mulligan cried.

"Alive!" De Cade amended. "I want the privilege of finishing him myself!"

Spraying lead fast and furious, Fargo gained the corner of the crew's quarters. If he had any say in the matter, what De Cade wanted and what De Cade was going to get were two different things. A river man breaking wide to the left drew his next shot. His target tumbled into a lifeless sprawl.

There was a lull as De Cade's men scrambled for cover. Fargo used it to reload, then moved around the texas to the narrow starboard gangway. Producing the Arkansas toothpick, he slashed the rope binding Jasmine's wrists. To his amazement, the second he did, she flung herself into his arms and planted a fevered kiss on his lips. He tried to pry her off but she insisted on lingering, on poking her tongue into his mouth and swirling it over his gums. Pushing harder, he separated them and whispered, "This is hardly the right time or place."

The redhead grinned coyly. "I just wanted to thank you properly for comin' back. I thought I was a goner."

"You still might be if you don't keep your mind on what we have to do," Fargo cautioned. Taking her hand, he whispered, "It's best to go for the high ground. We'll climb up on top of the texas."

"The what?"

Fargo could not spare the time to explain that the cabin housing the crew was so named because it was annexed to the upper deck much as Texas had once been annexed to the United States. He headed for the stairs that would take them to the top of the cabin. To reach them, he had to cross a short open space between the wall and the companionway.

Hot lead spurted from the vicinity of the starboard paddle wheel housing. Fargo replied in kind, and a man screamed in agony. Then they were racing up the steps, guns booming all over the upper deck. Fargo snapped off a couple of shots, aiming at gun flashes. They gained the cabin roof and dropped behind the rail.

All shooting ceased. Fargo replaced the spent cartridges before slinking along the rail until he was near the door to the wheelhouse. He broke for it, weaving as he ran, Jasmine mimicking him precisely. No gunfire erupted this time. Throwing the door open, he let her enter first.

The scent of tobacco filled the small room. Since the pilot needed a clear view of the river on all sides, the upper half of each wall was a wide window. The wheel itself stood near the front one. A small stove, a bench, and chairs were the only furniture.

Fargo prowled the windows, seeking the cutthroats. He spied a rifleman on top of the port paddle wheel housing, another by one of the towering smokestacks, still another behind a lifeboat. The rest were too well hidden.

Commotion at the companionway leading up from the middle deck caught his eye. Reinforcements had arrived in the form of two more crewmen. Others were bound to show up before long. He had to get Jasmine out of there before escape became impossible.

"Can you swim?" Fargo asked her.

"Are you kiddin'? All the years I've spent in the bayou, I can swim better than a tadpole." She paused. "Why? How can we reach the water? We're three decks up." She paused again. "You're not thinkin' of jumpin', are you? It's too shallow. We'd bust every bone in our bodies."

"Where there's a will," Fargo quipped, and walked over to a heavy cord that dangled from the bottom of what appeared to be a pipe inserted through the roof. Only it was not a pipe. The cord connected to the steamboat's powerful whistle. Since the boilers were not running, the whistle probably wouldn't work. Then again, there might be enough pressure left in the pipe for a few sustained bursts. He yanked on the cord.

A raucous blast of sound echoed from the bluffs and off across Baton Rouge.

"What did you do that for?" Jamine wanted to know.

"To keep De Cade on his toes. Maybe he'll think it was a signal," Fargo said. He moved around the wheelhouse collecting all the paper he could find. The pilot's log, a few books, a sheath of writing paper, and more. Piling his collection in the center, he stepped to the stove.

"What the dickens are you up to?"

Fargo opened the small door, picked up the poker leaning against the side, and poked in the coals. At the very bottom he found a few red embers that would do the job. Tongs enabled him to pick up the biggest ember and carry it over to the pile. "Open the window on the north side," he directed.

Jasmine quickly did so. "You're not fixin' to set the boat on fire, are you? The flames could jump to shore, and the whole blamed city might go up."

Fargo did not need to be reminded. Some years back, a fire had started on a moored steamboat in St. Louis and in no time had spread like a prairie wildfire. Twenty-three boats and fifteen city blocks had been destroyed.

But in this case it could not be helped. Fargo needed something to keep the crew busy while he whisked Jasmine out of there. By opening the window he insured that De Cade would see the smoke moments after the paper caught. That should give the crew plenty of forewarning.

Without hesitation Fargo placed the embers on the papers. The pile smoldered. Tiny flames licked at the sheets, growing larger rapidly. Stepping to the whistle, he pulled on the cord, setting it off again. But instead of letting go, he tied the end of the cord to a peg on the wall so that the whistle would blow until the pressure petered out.

Jasmine had her hands over her ears. "I can barely hear myself think!" she said.

That was the general idea. The whistle would bring flocks of curious down to the waterfront, adding to the confusion Fargo hoped to cause. He took her hand and dashed to the door. As they burst onto the roof of the texas, he heard De Cade bellow.

"Somebody shoot that whistle or we'll have the whole damn city down on us!"

Rifles cracked. In the dark the slender whistle proved a difficult target. It continued to wail as Fargo darted to the steps leading down to the upper deck. A bulky figure was just starting up them. The river man fired a fraction before Fargo, but Fargo was the one who did not miss.

Taking the steps two at a bound, Fargo flew to the bottom. His intention was to head forward and try to make his way to the lower deck, but as he came to the corner of the cabin, he spied five or six men making a concerted rush on the texas.

The only way out was aft. Whirling, Fargo sprinted toward the starboard paddle wheel. Just in time he remembered the rifleman perched on top. He looked up as the rifle boomed and lead bit into the boards at his feet. A stroke of the Colt jolted the shooter, who flung out his arms and pitched headfirst from his roost. His body hit with a loud splat. Fargo kept running.

The whistle faltered, gained steam again, warbled a few seconds, and expired.

"There they are! Get them!"

That sounded like Mulligan. Fargo pulled Jasmine around the housing as guns opened up from several directions. Slugs thudded like hail. He snapped off a shot at vague shadows.

"Wait! Look at the wheelhouse!" someone screeched above the gunfire. "Isn't that smoke?"

The firing stopped. Smoke was indeed pouring from the open window. In the sudden silence Jace De Cade's roar of outrage was like the bawl of a stricken grizzly. "Damn you, stranger, all to hell!" Feet clomped loudly. "Lacombe! Mulligan! Get up there and put that out or we're all dead men! Move it!"

Fargo continued aft. The fire would only keep the river men busy for a little while. He hurried past elevated skylights, past lifeboats, across a long open space to the stern rail. Here no cover existed. If they were caught, they would be gunned down in moments.

As if Jasmine sensed as much, she said, "We're doomed, aren't we?"

Not if Fargo could help it. Just below the rail was a derrick used to lower the rowboats. The boom jutted at a seventy-degree angle, supported by cables attached to the edge of the upper deck. Holstering the Colt, he hiked a leg and stepped over the rail, then offered his hand to the redhead.

Jasmine blinked. "Oh, God! You can't want me to do what I think you do."

"Would you rather die?"

145

Nervous as a hen that sees the shadow of a hawk, Jasmine climbed over and stood beside him, clinging to his arm. "This is insane."

Fargo slowly squatted and reached out to grip one of the thick support cables. "We'll go out to the boom," he told her, "then climb down to the lower deck." It sounded so easy, but doing it would not be. Sliding off the edge, he hung by both arms a moment to test the cable. It held. Moving hand over hand, he angled out to the large wooden pole. A pulley was the means by which the boats were lowered. To reach the lower deck, Fargo first had to crank the pulley to feed through the heavier cable that normally bore the weight of the rowboats.

Looping his legs around the boom to free his hands, Fargo set to work. It was arduous toil. The pulley had not been used in ages and resisted every tug. It creaked loudly with each turn.

All the while, over at the wheelhouse the river men were in an uproar. Flames licked at the roof. Thick winding coils of smoke curled skyward. Crewmen were running every which way, some bringing buckets of water, others wielding blankets and brooms. Above the din rose De Cade's commanding voice.

Fargo cranked until his hand was sore, yet the boom cable only lowered halfway down. He switched hands. Suddenly the support cable swayed, and he glanced over to find the redhead hanging by her hands.

"Someone is coming!" Jasmine whispered, and hastened toward him. She was scared but she never wavered. And she was smart enough not to look down.

Fargo cranked faster. The creaking grew louder. He watched the rail, hoping against hope that they had not been detected. It was in vain.

A river man appeared. He glanced to starboard and to port, puzzled by the creaks, not yet certain where they came from.

Forking his left arm over the boom, Fargo drew the Colt. He had to be careful not to drop it. The river man advanced. Almost to the rail, the man thought to look at the derrick. Shock registered. Fargo extended the pistol as the man brought up a rifle. The Colt bucked first, and the crewman clutched at his chest, folded in half, and keeled over the rail.

The body bounced off the middle deck on its way down. It hit the water with a tremendous splash.

Pounding steps alerted Fargo that more were on the way. Wedging the Colt under his gun belt, he started down the boom cable, saying, "Come on!" The thick rope was slippery, forcing him to wrap his legs around it to keep from losing his purchase. Quickly as possible, he descended to the end. It hung fifteen feet above the Mississippi and about five feet from the vessel.

"Look out!" Jasmine cried.

Two men were at the top deck railing. One elevated a rifle to take a hasty bead.

"Let go!" Fargo shouted, and did so. He broke the surface feet first, sinking in over his head. Somehow his hat stayed on. Stroking upward, he angled closer to the vessel so Jasmine would not land on him when she hit. He heard the splash of her impact at the same second he heard the rifle belch lead. Bullets zipped into the water within inches of his head.

Then Fargo was next to the *River Queen*, and the rifleman could not see him because of the overhang. Jasmine sputtered up within arm's reach. He pulled her to his side. "Are you hurt?"

"No," she coughed. "But what now?"

Fargo showed her. The log he had floated out on earlier was still there, held fast against the steamboat by the current. Draping an arm over one end, he had her grab the other. "We'll head out into the river and drift until we're safe," he proposed.

"Whenever you're ready."

Kicking off from the side of the vessel, Fargo stroked toward the middle of the broad Mississippi. The river man on the upper deck banged off two shots that narrowly missed. As the darkness closed around them, the man stopped firing. Fargo smiled at Jasmine. It would not be long now before they were back on land. He would take her to the livery and head out at first light for Possum Hollow. In a few days she would be back with Constance and Jessie, where she belonged.

A lot of yelling came from the riverboat. Judging by the scant amount of smoke that rose from the wheelhouse, the fire had been extinguished. Jace De Cade had saved his pride and joy.

"You did it," Jasmine said.

Fargo felt something brush against the back of his leg and creep between his thighs. For a harrowing moment he mistook it for a snake or a snapper. But it was the redhead's foot. He had to smile. Women never ceased to astound him. There they were, barely safe ten seconds, and she was hinting at what she had in mind for later. "Behave yourself," he growled.

"Spoilsport."

Twisting, Fargo glanced at her just as a new sound intruded on the night, the dull throb of a steamboat's engines being turned over. He saw men undo the mooring lines at the bow of the *River Queen,* saw ripples slowly spread from under the nearest paddle wheel. A shiver ran down his spine as he realized the significance. Not a shiver of fear, but a shiver of dread for the woman he brashly assumed he had rescued.

"What is it?" Jasmine asked, then turned to see for herself. "What in the world! Why are they putting out at this time of night?" She faced him, comprehension draining the blood from her face. "Dear Lord! De Cade is coming after us! He intends to run us down!"

"Kick harder," Fargo urged, his mind racing. Their salvation lay in reaching land, but they were five hundred feet from the nearest shore and would have to fight the current every foot of the way. He turned the log anyway, pumping his legs, his free arm stroking cleanly.

The *River Queen* eased into the river, her paddles gaining speed as her boilers built up steam. The great vessel began to swing around to bring her bow into the current.

Fargo was trying his utmost to make straight for land, but the strong current worked against them. For every yard they traveled toward shore, the current carried them a yard farther down the river. For over a minute they struggled valiantly but made slight headway.

Meanwhile the *River Queen* had almost swung around. In a short while the riverboat would get under way under a full head of steam. When that happened, it would be on them with the swiftness of an attacking alligator.

Jasmine started to flounder. "I can't keep this up!" she said. "My dress is hamperin' me too much."

Fargo stopped swimming. "Quit trying," he instructed her. "We'll let the current carry us for a while."

Now that they were not resisting the flow, the log shot off down the waterway faster than their combined strength could have propelled it. All they had to do was hang on as it made for the first bend below Baton Rouge. Fargo began to think that they might actually escape after all. Then he shifted to check on the riverboat.

Billowing smoke from both chimneys, huge paddle wheels churning, the *River Queen* skimmed the surface at a speed that belied her bulk. Lights had flared the length of her decks. At the bow were six or seven men holding long poles. At the end of each hung a bright lantern.

"Maybe they won't spot us," Jasmine said.

"Maybe." But Fargo was not very confident. The log was pale gray. It would stand out like a white handkerchief against a black coat. He kicked to go faster.

They were close to the bend when a rifle spat gun smoke on the steamboat's upper deck. A tiny splash occurred a few dozen feet to the rear. The marksman had undershot, but a few more tries and he would get their range.

Fargo saw that Jasmine was slipping. She clutched at the top of the log. It was so slick that she could not hang on. As she started to go under, Fargo dropped back, snared her, and clamped his other arm securely. She molded herself to him, trembling slightly, whether from fright or the cold water he could not say.

The log sailed around the turn, the current bearing it toward the opposite shoreline. Fargo helped it along by using both legs. But they still went much too slowly to suit him.

A keening blast of the whistle heralded the steamboat, which swept around the wide bend at her top speed, white froth spewing from under her paddle wheels. De Cade was giving her everything she had. The combined light from the lanterns formed a false moon on the river's surface, a moon that swelled toward the log as the riverboat closed in.

Fargo refused to give up. He held Jasmine and his own body close to the side to reduce drag. His flailing boots added momentum, until all of a sudden his leg ankle slammed against something that rippled pain clear up his leg. It had been a snag of some sort, either a submerged tree or rocks. He pushed against the log to change course, then realized the mistake he was making and stuck to the same heading. A long, thin object poked out of the river to his left. Going by, he learned it was part of a limb.

Inwardly Fargo tingled with excitement. De Cade's mistakes were about to catch up with him. Running the Mississippi at night was risky unless the pilot stayed in the open water at the center. The snag-studded shallows were a hazard even in broad daylight.

The current slackened. Fargo shoved the log aside and swam, holding onto Jasmine. Her clothes had become so waterlogged that she could barely stay afloat. They were one hundred feet from a reed-choked bank. He concentrated on that and that alone, his limbs flying, his chest expanding with every breath he sucked into his lungs. The whistle sounded again, much closer than before. Fargo cast a look back.

Jace De Cade stood on the lower deck alongside the men holding the lanterns. Someone handed him a rifle, which he raised to his shoulder. He was grinning as he settled the sights on Fargo and the redhead, grinning as he thumbed back the hammer.

Fargo swore that De Cade was looking him right in the eyes when the *River Queen* struck the snag. The bow of the boat crumpled like so much paper, scattering crewmen right and left like chaff in the wind. De Cade was one of those who went flying. The steamboat listed, the ripping and rending of wood drowning out the yells and wails of the crew. Her ruptured bow canted, revealed a gaping hole in the bottom. Yet for all the damage, the riverboat hurtled on toward the shore.

Directly in its path were Fargo and Jasmine. He exerted himself to his limit, swimming furiously, seeking to reach the bank before the steamboat plowed into them. The crippled juggernaut loomed steadily nearer. Fire had broken out and was spreading rapidly. A man screamed hysterically.

Fargo veered to the right. His arms were so tired that he could barely lift them. His legs were as sluggish as maple syrup. Jasmine had her arms around his neck, further weighing him down. On the brink of exhaustion, he had to stop. His feet brushed bottom.

At least one of the steamboat's engines was still running. The vessel had tilted so sharply that her crew had to grab onto whatever they could to prevent being dumped in the water. One man, ablaze from head to toe, leaped to the rail on the middle deck and vaulted into the Mississippi. He disappeared with a hiss.

It did not cheer Fargo to realize that the *River Queen* would miss them. There was a new threat now, one that could prove equally as fatal. Sliding his arms under Jasmine's, he heaved landward. "Run!" he told her. "If you value your life, you have to move!"

With a resounding crunch, the *River Queen* smashed into another snag. The impact caused her to shake violently from the jack staff to the aft derrick. Her bow partially rose into the air, timbers and beams falling from her like scales from a shedding serpent. She slammed into shore south of the bank, digging a deep furrow as she barreled through dense brush and into a stand of trees. The oaks and maples finally brought her to a stop.

Fargo saw men scrambling frantically to get off their doomed mistress. He lifted Jasmine from her feet and rushed the last five yards. Just as they set foot on solid ground, the *River Queen*'s boilers exploded.

13

Once, years ago, a steamboat by the name of the *Saluda* went up like a keg of black powder. A third of the vessel disintegrated, and the rest was reduced to twisted wreckage. What made the event memorable to Skye Fargo was hearing that the six-hundred-pound safe had been blown two hundred yards from the river. It bore home the point that when boilers exploded, they turned the ships in which they were housed into gigantic bombs and everything on the riverboats into lethal shrapnel.

That was why Fargo threw Jasmine Tanner to the dank earth when the *River Queen* was rent to ribbons. He flung himself on top of her, shielding Jasmine with his own body, an arm over his head to afford what protection it could. Through a crack where his elbow bent, he saw the bulk of the steamboat blown in a million different directions. Fully half the ship was pulverized in the time it would take to inhale. A crewman who had reached land turned to see the devastation and was torn in half by a flying boiler flue. Another had his forehead crushed by the impact of a chunk of molten iron.

The rain of debris seemed to last forever. Fargo was pelted by bits and pieces without letup. Wood, metal, glass, even body parts pattered down. None, thankfully, were big enough to inflict harm. A choking cloud of dust and mist limited visibility for a while but soon settled.

When Fargo was convinced that the worst was over, he rose onto his knees and helped Jasmine up. She gawked at the destruction. A severed leg that bobbed on the water nearby made her cover her mouth and double over.

Nothing moved among the wreckage. Not a living soul had apparently survived. Standing, Fargo moved along the shore, seeing blistered corpses here, ravaged bodies there. He stopped counting at nine. At one spot was a jumble of limbs and heads, but no torsos. He saw an arm clothed in expensive black material and thought it might be Jace De Cade's.

"Please, Skye," Jasmine said. "Take me away from here. I can't stand this much longer."

Fargo clasped her hand and headed into a grove of willows. Twenty yards from the river he spotted a figure propped against a tree, as if waiting to pounce on them. He flourished the Colt and moved in front of the redhead. Then he discovered that the figure was headless. Even so, he recognized who it was thanks to a bullwhip coiled around the right shoulder.

"Mulligan!" Jasmine exclaimed. Suddenly she stormed over to the body and kicked it in the groin so hard that it toppled, the arms flapping. "That was for the times he beat me, and for threatenin' to kill my ma and Jessie if I didn't go along with what they wanted."

Fury claimed her. Fury, and the whole storm of emotions she had pent up since being abducted. She kicked the body over and over, stopping only when her emotions were spent. Her entire shapely figure quaking, she crossed her arms and said in a small voice, "I'm so cold all of a sudden. How about you?"

Her chills had nothing to do with her feelings. It was the result of being soaked for so long. Fargo had lived in the wilds long enough to know that a person should never take such chills lightly. Abnormal lowering of the body temperature could bring on pneumonia and other illnesses. In some cases, it even brought on death. "I'm used to it," he told her.

Steering the redhead into a clearing, Fargo had her sit on a log while he swiftly gathered wood. Since he did not have his saddlebags handy, he could not rely on his steel and flint to get the fire going. Nor could he make a bow drill with the whangs on his buckskins so wet. He did it the old-fashioned way, by finding a long, straight stick and spinning it like a fire drill in a notch in the log.

Kindling was no problem. Fargo scaled a tree to raid a long abandoned bird nest. In short order he had flames crackling and fed them dead branches until they were knee-high.

Jasmine was staring toward the Mississippi. "Maybe someone in Baton Rouge will send a boat out and see our fire. We could be back before midnight."

"I wouldn't get my hopes up," Fargo advised. No one would dare bring a boat in close to where the *River Queen* snagged until daylight for fear of suffering her fate. "You need to get out of those clothes."

The redhead had been looking perfectly miserable. Now she beamed and said in a sultry tone, "Why, Mr. Fargo, you randy devil you! After all we just went through, you're still rarin' to go. I like that in a man."

Fargo laughed. He slapped his leg and vented a ripsnorting belly laugh the likes of which he had not done in years. She stared at him as if he had been hit on the head during the blast.

"Whatever is that all about?"

"I doubt I could explain," Fargo said, removing his hat and setting it on the log close to the fire. Next he began to peel off his shirt. It clung to him like a second skin, resisting every tug. When he got it over his head, he saw that Jasmine was undoing the top of her dress. "Need some help?"

The redhead's luscious lips quirked. "My, ever the gallant gentleman." She wriggled seductively. "I suppose it would help me warm up that much faster, wouldn't it?" Holding her arms out, she said, "Where do you want to start, handsome?"

Squatting, Fargo finished unfastening the clasps and buttons. There were so many that he was at it for minutes, Jasmine smirking at him every second.

"I did it on purpose, you know," she commented.

"Did what?"

"Picked the hardest dress in the world to take off. I figured that if some old drunk was going to paw me, I wasn't going to make it easy for him."

The front parted. "Their loss," Fargo said, slipping his hands under the material to cover her swelling mounds. Her skin was cold to the touch, dotted with goose bumps. As he massaged she slowly warmed, her nipples thrusting into his palms.

"Ummmmmmm," Jasmine breathed, closing her eyes. "You have very nimble fingers. I'd say you've done this sort of thing before."

"Once or twice," Fargo allowed, lowering his hands to her ribs. They were ice, as was the lower part of her back. He rubbed and rubbed. She licked her lips a few times and once let out with a low moan.

"Keep this up and I'll be hotter than the fire," Jasmine joked, parting her legs so he could move closer. "I'm afraid you won't get any sleep tonight."

Fargo found her navel and ran a finger around the lip. "I'll live," he said.

It was not Jasmine who responded. It was someone behind him, someone whose voice rang of vindictive spite. "Think so, do you, *monsieur?* Somehow we doubt it."

Spinning, Fargo dropped his hand to his Colt, but froze with the draw uncompleted. Henri Lacombe had a Sharps trained on his chest. Beside the Cajun, cane in hand, as dapper as ever even though dripping wet, stood his employer.

"I can't tell you how much this pleases me," Jace De Cade said. "A fitting touch of irony, wouldn't you agree? How kind of the fates to spare the two people I most want to see suffer." Stepping to the right, he wagged the cane. "This really is too wonderful for words."

Lacombe was feasting his eyes on Jasmine's exposed charms. "I do hope I get to indulge before you finish them off, boss. It would be a shame to waste such a fine woman, no?"

"Is that all you ever think of?" De Cade said testily. Before the Cajun could reply, he went on, "I've just lost a steamboat that cost me more than you'll ever make in your lifetime, every last man except the two of us perished, my gala was a disaster, and all you care about is indulging yourself with this bayou harlot?"

Lacombe chuckled. "You must forgive me, *monsieur*. Wine, women, and nights of passion are what I live for."

De Cade glared at Jasmine. "This woman has cost me dearly. I intend to see that she pays just as dearly. You can dally with females all you want once we get back to Baton Rouge."

"As you wish, *monsieur*," Lacombe said, sounding disappointed.

Fargo had not taken his eyes off the Sharps. If the Cajun lowered the barrel for just an instant, he was going to draw. The scrape of steel on wood, though, made him glance at De Cade.

The ivory eagle at the end of the cane was actually the hilt of a concealed sword. De Cade brandished it in a deft flurry and adopted a stance Fargo had seen fencing masters use. The slender tip lanced at his neck but only pricked the skin, a superb display of De Cade's control.

"You will hand me the Colt, butt first. Use two fingers."

As Fargo began to comply, the tip pierced him another fraction.

"Do it slowly or I will run you through."

Fargo had no doubts about that. Gingerly he slid the pistol clear. Out of the corner of an eye he noticed Jasmine. She was in shock at the sudden turn of events and had not even bothered to cover herself. Which was too bad. If she'd had her wits about her and thought to distract the two killers, the ordeal would be over. Against his better judgment he let the Colt be taken.

De Cade stepped back and smiled. "Now I can take my sweet time," he said. Tucking the revolver under his belt, he swirled the sword in small circles near Fargo's face. "I just don't know where to begin. What do you think, Henri? Should I put out his eyes first? Or perhaps open his wrists?"

Lacombe still had not let the Sharps dip. "If it were me, I wouldn't blind him, boss. I'd want him to see what I was doing."

"An excellent suggestion," De Cade agreed. "His suffering will be greater that way."

While they talked, Fargo inched his right hand to the top edge of his right boot. His fingers probed and found the hilt to the Arkansas toothpick. He dug his heels into the ground, preparing to spring, then was as startled as the other two men when an anguished wail tore from Jasmine Tanner's throat.

"No!" she screamed, leaping to her feet. "I won't make it easy on you! I won't be slaughtered like a helpless lamb!" Pivoting, she bounded into the brush, her dress opening wide as she turned to reveal her ample bosom.

Henri Lacombe automatically aligned the rifle with her back and was about to fire when De Cade called out.

"Don't shoot! I want her alive! Go fetch the fool while I tend to our friend here."

Sighing, the Cajun ran off.

De Cade stepped back and leveled his sword at Fargo. "There is one thing I would like to know before I begin. Who are you working for?"

Fargo opened his mouth, but was cut off.

"Don't lie. I wasn't born yesterday. You didn't go to all this trouble for that pathetic tramp. Someone sent you, and

I want to know who." De Cade leaned intently forward. "Are you an agent for the federal government, as I've suspected all along? Or is it the state? Or perhaps one of my old enemies hired you?"

"You're right," Fargo said, shifting slightly so his arm would not be obstructed by his hip. "I am doing this for someone else."

"I knew it!" De Cade crowed. "Who?"

"A ten-year-old girl."

De Cade looked as if he had just sat on a broomstick. "What? How gullible do you think I am?"

"It's Jasmine's little sister, Jessie. She wrote me a letter asking that I track Jasmine down."

The truth of it sank in. Jace De Cade straightened, blank with astonishment. "A ten-year-old girl?" he repeated in stunned disbelief, staring toward the Mississippi and what was left of his elegant steamboat. "All this because of a *child?*"

Fargo nodded. As he did, he pushed to his feet and swept the toothpick up and out, throwing it straight at De Cade's heart. It was a flawless toss. He would have slain the man on the spot had that slender sword not flicked in a precise counter. The toothpick went flying. He heard it clatter against the log, but he did not look to see where it had fallen. He could not. For De Cade turned the parry into a thrust.

Fargo skipped aside as the sword speared at his chest. It missed by a whisker. Dancing backward, he evaded two wide slashes and a stab at his groin.

De Cade was smiling as if there were something he knew that Fargo did not. "Agile, aren't you?" he taunted. "Not that it will do you any good. I've been the champion of the Rosileau Fencing Academy for five years running. Last spring I placed third at the state tournament."

"Only third?" Fargo could not resist saying, and had to dodge several thrusts and cuts that would have inflicted major wounds.

Stepping back, De Cade swished a figure eight in the air. "The last fool who stood up to me had his tongue cut out before he was wrapped in chains and dumped alive in the river. But this way is better. I get to watch you die a piece at a time." Suddenly bending at the right knee, he drove the sword forward.

Fargo nearly tripped getting out of the way. He backed up until a limb gouged him in the back, letting him know that he was at the edge of the clearing.

"Nowhere left to go," De Cade sneered. "What a pity." He attacked with redoubled vigor, his arm always in motion, never allowing a moment's rest.

Backpedaling, Fargo ducked and dodged and weaved. Time and again he narrowly missed being transfixed. Time and again he came close to being slashed wide open. He circled the clearing without being aware he had done so until he bumped into the log. It brought him up short.

De Cade paused. He was breathing heavily now, and his wrist had lost some of its quickness. "I've never met anyone with reflexes like yours," he said. "You're more cat than human."

Fargo did not waste breath talking. Poised on the balls of his feet, he awaited the next onslaught. It was not long in coming.

"Die!" De Cade roared, and threw everything he had into a lightning thrust. In his desire to end the clash, he overextended himself, thrusting farther than ever.

A simple twist and Fargo was spared. He saw the steel flash past his chest. His fingers closed on De Cade's wrist, and he swung to the right, throwing out his leg so that it caught De Cade across the shins and tripped him. De Cade, cursing up a storm, attempted to wrench free and stand, but Fargo dived, tackling him around the waist and bearing both of them to the ground.

De Cade fought in a frenzy. He punched. He kicked. He

yanked on his sword arm. He even tried to ram his forehead into Fargo's face.

Rolling back and forth, grappling savagely, they came up against the log. Fargo found himself pinned between it and De Cade with De Cade partially on top. Unable to gain enough leverage to hurl the man, he locked his hand on De Cade's wrist to hold the sword at bay. By gradual degrees the tip inched toward his left eye.

"I've got you now!" De Cade gloated.

Just then, from the surrounding forest, came a scream of mortal terror. It was so loud, and so close, that Jace De Cade inadvertently glanced up.

Heaving upward, Fargo snapped the crown of his head into the underside of De Cade's jaw. There was a loud crack, and De Cade scrambled backward, blood seeping from his mouth. Fargo slid to the left to put some distance between them and his hand nearest the log pressed down on a familiar object.

Shaking his head to clear it, De Cade rose to his knees. He spat blood, and glared. "I no longer want to whittle you down. I just want you dead. Period." Flinging erect, he adopted a guard posture. His eyes narrowed, he took a half step, and sheared his weapon in for the kill.

Fargo anticipated the move. He brought the toothpick around, swatting the tip of the sword aside, then pumped his legs upward, slicing the knife into De Cade below the sternum.

Jace De Cade jerked backward, stupefied, not quite certain what had been done until his gaze fell on the bloody toothpick. He looked down at himself, at the spreading dark stain. His arms went limp. The sword fell. "I'll be damned," he said, and gave Fargo a peculiar look. "A ten-year-old girl, you say? Who would have thought it?" Like a house of cards folding in on itself, so folded the most powerful man in Baton Rouge.

Fargo rolled the body over and reclaimed his Colt. It had been De Cade's final mistake not to use it. Sticking the toothpick under his belt for the time being, he sprinted into the woods in the direction the scream came from. Covering twenty yards, he halted to listen. In the distance an alligator bellowed. Along the river frogs croaked. A few crickets chirped. That was all.

Heading inland, Fargo stopped every ten or fifteen yards. He made no more noise than the wind. He heard nothing out of the ordinary. As best he could figure, Jasmine had found someplace to hide and the crafty Cajun was lying low until she broke from cover. He would have called out. But if Lacombe was closer to her when she answered, her life would be forfeited. ·

Fargo came to an oak tree. A thicket to the south rustled, and he distinguished a figure creeping away from it. He took aim as best he could. When the figure uncoiled, he was ready, but he did not shoot. The darkness could not hide the swirling mane of hair. "Jasmine!" he whispered.

To the southeast Lacombe's rifle thundered. A heavy slug smacked into the tree trunk next to Fargo's shoulder. He answered with a pair of shots, but it was impossible to say whether he scored. Darting to a bush half as tall as he was, he dropped onto his knees.

Jasmine had disappeared again. Fargo relied on her being smart enough not to move until he had finished with Lacombe. Or the other way around. Lowering onto his belly, he crawled toward the thicket. At that moment the Cajun would be changing position, too. Yet Fargo scanned the vegetation again and again without turning up any sign of him.

For a while Fargo lay as still as a stone. He had about convinced himself that the only way to flush Lacombe was to loop to the southwest and back again to come up on him from the rear when a twig cracked. A bush shook, followed by a muffled outcry. Then the night was quiet once again. But not for long.

"Do you hear me, *mon ami?*"

The shout came from near the bush. Fargo raised the Colt, anxious for a glimpse.

"I have something you care about," Lacombe yelled. "Or should I say *someone* you care about." The high weeds shook. A resounding slap rang out.

"He's not lyin'!" Jasmine Tanner hollered. "But it doesn't much matter what happens to me. Don't listen to anything he says."

Another slap ended her statement. Fargo snaked to the right along the bottom of the thicket, where it would be hardest for the Cajun to catch sight of him. They still could come out on top if he could work his way around behind Lacombe.

"Listen well, *tigre.* You will step out into the open with your arms over your head or I will gut your pretty friend like a fish. *Comprenez-vous?*"

Fargo hesitated. To do as the Cajun wanted was the same as asking to be shot. To refuse meant that Jasmine's life span could be measured in seconds instead of years.

"I will count to three. If you have not stood up, so be it. I have misjudged how you feel about this *fille.* Which is too bad for her, *non?*" Lacombe paused. *"Un. Deux."*

When all was said and done, Fargo could no more allow Jasmine to die than he could voluntarily stop breathing. Sliding the Colt behind him, under his belt, he hoisted his arms and slowly rose. "I've done it," he said in case the Cajun had not spotted him. "Don't hurt her."

A nasty laugh preceded Lacombe as he roughly shoved Jasmine into the open. He was not carrying the Sharps. His right hand was next to her neck, and in it was clutched the special blade he carried up his sleeve. "You have a soft heart, *monsieur.* That is a luxury men like us cannot afford."

Fargo let them come to him. He bent his elbows so his hands were only as high as his shoulders. To stall for time, he said, "Your boss is dead. Why go through with this?"

"Need you ask?" Lacombe responded. "It was either you or me from the moment we met." Yanking Jasmine to a standstill, he gripped her hair and pulled her head back, further exposing her pale throat. "You should never have stuck your nose into our business."

Jasmine tried to pull loose and received a brutal shaking for her effort.

"Behave, *ma petite*," Lacombe scolded. "You will live a little longer if you do." He glanced at Fargo's belt. "Where is your pistol?"

"I dropped it back there," Fargo said, nodding at the thicket. "I didn't think you wanted me to have it on me when I showed myself."

Lacombe smirked. "How considerate of you. If I was an idiot, I would believe you. Since I am not, do me a favor and slowly turn around."

Fargo glanced at Jasmine. Was it his imagination, or was the firming of her jaw a sign that she knew what had to be done? He started to rotate, never taking his eyes off her. When she raised her right foot, he was ready. Lacombe drew back, then tensed his arm to stab her. Fargo was faster. His first shot smashed the Cajun in the chest. His second tottered the Cajun against a tree. His third brought the Cajun crashing down.

The redhead ran to him, her arms slipping around his chest, her lips showering kisses on his mouth and cheeks. "You did it! You saved me again! How can I ever thank you enough?"

Skye Fargo smiled. "I know a way."

LOOKING FORWARD!
The following is the opening
section fom the next novel in the exciting
Trailsman series from Signet:

THE TRAILSMAN #184
ROCKY MOUNTAIN NIGHTMARE

*1861, high up in the Rockies, where if a man wasn't
careful, all that
thin air might have him seeing things . . .*

The raging snowstorm struck without warning.

For the better part of an hour Skye Fargo had been toil-
ing up a steep slope choked with firs and deadfalls. The few
glimpses he caught of the sky showed patches of bright
blue and fluffy clouds. He had no inkling of the terrible
tantrum Nature was about to throw.

Then the big man in buckskins rode out of the trees onto
a barren, jagged spine high atop the towering Rocky Mountains. He reined up so his weary Ovaro could rest.

Shifting in the saddle, Fargo caught a blast of frigid air
full in the face. Squinting his lake-blue eyes, he was startled to see a massive bank of roiling gray clouds sweeping
in from the west. Already the storm front was on the other
side of the valley he had just crossed. It would be on him in
minutes.

Swearing luridly, the Trailsman applied his spurs. The pinto stallion, sensing his unease, trotted along the spine to where a narrow game trail wound down from the lofty heights.

Fargo's lips tightened. Made by mountain sheep, mule deer, elk, and bear, the trail was no wider than his broad shoulders. Worse, in many places it was flanked by sheer cliffs. A single misstep would spell doom.

Yet Fargo had no choice but to descend and seek cover. The temperature was dropping rapidly. Caught in the open, he would be battered by the merciless elements.

There was no telling how many men had lost their lives to the high country's notoriously fickle weather. Scores, maybe. Men who, like Fargo, were caught flat-footed by raging storms that swept out of nowhere to engulf them in blinding sheets of snow and ice.

Fargo kneed the Ovaro down the trail. Its hooves sent small stones clattering over a precipice. Leaning out, Fargo saw the bottom, strewn with boulders, over a thousand feet below. He shuddered to think of the consequences should he follow those stones down.

Howling like a banshee, the wind grew stronger by the moment. It buffeted Fargo and the pinto, forcing him to pull his hat down around his ears and hunch his shoulders against the gale. A few flakes of snow danced in the air like tiny white fireflies. They were harbingers of the swarm to come.

Rounding a bend, Fargo rose in the stirrups to scan the mountainside. Another valley beckoned far, far below. But it would take as long to reach it as it had taken to climb to the ridge. By then the full force of the snowstorm would be unleashed.

The trail wound haphazardly toward a spur of rock that cut off Fargo's view of whatever lay beyond. A rush of icy wind brought goose bumps to his flesh. More and more flakes cavorted wildly in the rarefied atmosphere, almost as if they were taunting him. A few landed on his neck and hands, melting instantly, their cold touch a promise of the icy death that would be his if he was not careful.

Fargo came to the rock spur. As he went around it, the storm hit with all the elemental fury of an airborne tidal wave. Shrieking wind pummeled the peaks. A thick white blanket engulfed him. It became so cold that he could see puffs of his breath.

All was not lost, though. In the few seconds before the storm swallowed him whole, Fargo spotted a broad tableland several hundred feet lower. It had to be a half mile wide. Pines offered a safe haven, if only he could reach them.

Fargo abruptly stiffened, doubting his sanity. In the center of the tableland reared what appeared to be an immense man-made structure. He blinked against the driving snow, raising a hand to shield his eyes for a better look.

The raging white sheet closed around him like a glove. Fargo could not see his palm at arm's length, let alone the tableland. He shook his head, certain his eyes had deceived him. By his best reckoning he was sixty or seventy miles west of Denver, deep in the heart of the Rockies. Other than a few scattered mining camps, the region was uninhabited.

Except for roving bands of marauding Utes, of course.

Fargo forged on, holding the stallion to a slow walk, stopping often to bend down. The trail had narrowed. On his left loomed a rock wall; on his right the sheer drop-off. He had counted at least two more bends before he reached the tableland, but he could not be sure of exactly where they were.

It was a nightmare, that descent. What should have taken ten minutes took over an hour. Twice the Ovaro slipped, and each time Fargo's heart leaped into his throat as he felt the pinto start to go over the side. In each instance it regained its footing, snorting and quivering with fright.

All the while the storm roared and fumed around them, lashing them with snow and wind and cold. Since it was only early fall, Fargo had not brought a coat along. Until the storm appeared, the weather had been extremely mild. So much so that at night Fargo had lain under the sparkling stars with no blanket to cover him.

Now Fargo wished that he could take the time to unfasten his bedroll and wrap himself in a blanket or two. He was freezing. His buckskins were half-soaked, his skin a sheen of ice. His teeth took to chattering. Clamping them tight, he hunched forward to ward off the driving wind. It did no good.

Just when Fargo's nerves were frayed to the breaking point, the stallion nickered and bobbed its head. The rock wall to the left of them was gone. Cautiously, Fargo dismounted, to discover that they had finally reached the tableland.

Leading the pinto, Fargo trudged toward a dim, dark wall that had to be the forest. He clasped his arms to his chest for added warmth. The wind screamed shrilly, as if outraged that he would soon be safe.

Suddenly Fargo halted. Cocking his head, he listened intently. It had to be his imagination, because the scream that he was hearing sounded as if it issued from an inhuman throat. He shook his head, amused by his foolishness. No animals would be out in such foul weather. Grizzlies, mountain lions, and wolves would all be lying low until the worst was past. Just as he should be doing.

Tramping on through snow that was six inches deep and growing deeper by the minute, Fargo was overjoyed when somber ranks of pines loomed in front of him. Relieved, he entered the woodland. He paused to remove his hat and slap snow from his shoulders.

Here the worst of the tempest was blunted. The snow still fell thickly, but he could see for a dozen feet or so. And the wind was quieter, its icy bite no more than an annoying sting.

Smiling, Fargo put his hat back on, then froze in the act of adjusting the brim. From out of the pines on his left rose the same piercing scream he had heard earlier. This time there could be no doubt that it was not the wind. It was a living creature, but its scream was unlike any Fargo had ever heard.

Automatically, Fargo's right hand dropped to the butt of his Colt. He glanced at the Ovaro, which stood with ears pricked and nostrils flaring, staring into the dense growth that surrounded them. Something was definitely out there. *But what?*

Fargo was not superstitious by nature. Many Indian tribes believed the wilds were home to all sorts of spirits and unearthly creatures, but he had never been one to believe in something unless he saw it with his own eyes.

His scalp prickling, Fargo went on. He made no sound that could be heard above the wind, but the dull thud of the stallion's hooves were bound to attract whatever was out there. And they did.

Without warning a shape materialized at the limits of Fargo's vision. Dumbfounded, he stopped.

A tall, thin figure swayed on two spindly legs, its features blurred by the whipping white curtain. Lean arms lifted as if it were about to spring, and from its lips burst that horrid scream, only now the scream held a new note, a note of bloodthirsty rage.

Fargo's Colt leaped clear. His thumb curled the hammer back. Just as his finger began to caress the trigger, the eerie apparition vanished. He glanced to either side, thinking that it might circle and come at him from a different direction. Tense minutes passed, but the creature did not reappear.

Warily, Fargo hiked deeper into the forest. Above and around him the trees were being whipped ferociously. Limbs bent and creaked. Many snapped and cracked. It was impossible to pinpoint the screaming devil that he was sure stalked him.

A thicket materialized. Rather than go around, Fargo plowed into the cover, which rose as high as his chest.

Whatever was out there would not be able to get at him, he thought. But he was wrong.

He found out when the stallion whinnied and shied. A feral snarl explained why. Claws raked Fargo's left leg. Instinctively he jumped to the right.

A dim bulk was crouched at the base of a bush. It howled like a demented wolf, slashing fiercely at the pinto, which lurched backward just as Fargo was going to fire.

Yanked off balance, it was all Fargo could do to hold onto the reins. The figure flowed back into the gloom that had spawned it as Fargo fought to keep the pinto from fleeing in panic.

Another savage screech proved too much for the Ovaro. Nickering and bucking, it tore loose and bolted. The crash of undergrowth was the only way Fargo had of marking its flight.

He gave chase. To be stranded afoot in the wilderness was a death warrant for most. For a frontiersman of his caliber, for someone who had lived among Indians and knew how to live off the land as well as they did, it would not be as bad. But he would be lucky to reach Denver alive.

Heedless of the lurker in the storm, Fargo ran as fast as the terrain allowed. He weaved among trunks. He vaulted logs. He barreled through tracts of heavy brush. In his ears hissed the wind. The snow had tapered, though not by much.

A boulder the size of a log cabin barred his path, and Fargo raced on around. Out of the corner of his right eye he saw a shadow detach itself and surge toward him. Before he could halt or turn, the thing attacked.

A heavy body slammed into Fargo's back. The jarring impact knocked him to his hands and knees. Claws seared into his neck. He twisted, and suddenly realized that the claws were not really claws at all. He could feel the pressure of fingers and thumbs gouging into his flesh.

The claws were fingernails! Nails as long as the talons of birds of prey, as sharp as the fangs of cougars.

Fargo wrenched around, or tried to, but the figure clung to him with ghoulish strength. The nails dug deeper, drawing blood that froze almost as quickly as it oozed out. He flailed his elbows back and in, connecting with iron ribs. It elicited a screech of raw fury, but the wraith did not let go.

Frantically, Fargo threw himself from side to side. His beastly assailant snarled, and those awful fingers dug deeper. Then, by chance more than design, Fargo collided with a tree. Pivoting, he slammed his attacker against the bole, again and again.

The fourth time was the charm. Yowling like a rabid coyote, the apparition released him. Fargo spun, leveling the Colt. But as he brought the pistol up, the figure whirled and leaped like a two-legged bobcat. Steel-spring muscles carried it into undergrowth eight feet away.

Panting from his exertion, stung and sore and bleeding, Fargo ran to the same spot. The man was gone. He turned every which way, seeking some sign, but the snow and the vegetation conspired to thwart him.

A baffled oath burst from the Trailsman's lips. His trigger finger literally itched to stroke the trigger. He dashed a few yards into the trees, drawing up short when the futility of what he was trying to do impressed itself on him.

Backing to the boulder, Fargo resumed his search for the Ovaro. During the brief struggle he had been unable to tell if his attacker was white or red. Why the man wanted to kill him, he had no idea. He suspected that the mysterious stalker was somewhere nearby, waiting for an opportunity to try again.

How far Fargo ran, he could not say. Maybe two hundred yards. The wind slackened but the snow thickened, severely limiting visibility.

Fargo stopped to catch his breath. The moment he did, a vague ghastly specter rushed shrieking from the pines, ramming into him with frightening speed. Bowled over, his arms pinned against his body, Fargo felt teeth rake his neck. The wildman was striving to tear open his jugular!

Horror goaded Fargo into twisting and thrashing like a madman. His left arm broke free. He rained punches on the figure's head, but he might as well have been striking the ground. The growling, snapping figure held on.

They must have rolled over the brink of a knoll, because the next thing Fargo knew, they tumbled down a short slope littered with sharp rocks. At the bottom a boulder brought them to a stop.

For once luck worked in Fargo's favor. The wildman bore the brunt. Screeching like a stricken catamount, the man shoved upright and fled, favoring his left leg. Fargo rose to his knees and took a hasty bead, but not quite hasty enough. Once again the apparition disappeared before he could fire.

Fargo's hat had fallen off. Groping about, he found it and smacked it against his leg to shed snow. Circling the boulder, he moved off in a crouch. He was actually glad when the storm worsened. Every bit of extra cover helped.

His right boot bumped something. Stooping lower, he figured to find a large rock or a limb. Instead, his probing fingers roved over the stump of a sapling. The grooved surface told him that the tree had been chopped down, not blown over.

Indians would rather gather fallen branches than chop wood. They made their fires so small that an armful lasted all night.

Odds were, then, that whoever had cut down the sapling was white. Perhaps a prospector had staked a claim in the area, or an old trapper had a cabin nearby. Neither would explain the unprovoked attack.

Mystified, Fargo stalked on, always on the alert. He had covered a quarter of a mile when the wind tapered to a low moan and the snow dwindled to steady but widely spaced flakes. It was either a lull in the storm, or it was smaller in size and scope than he had reckoned.

Fargo could distinguish individual trees and other land-marks. He hoped his attacker would come after him now, when he could see well enough to get off a clear shot, but the wildman had apparently given up. It was tempting to start a fire and rest a spell, but he pushed on after the Ovaro.

Drifting snow had erased whatever tracks the stallion made. Fargo constantly looked for sign, to no avail. A clear-ing spread out before him. There he paused, debating whether to cut straight across and expose himself to the phantom.

It was then that a new sound fluttered through the wood-land, a sound that shocked Fargo as much as the screams had earlier. He tossed his head, but he still heard it. He slapped his ear, but it was working just fine. He pinched himself to verify it was not a dream. He was wide awake.

Why, then, did he hear the musical lilt of a woman's throaty voice, humming gaily as if she did not have a single care in the world? It couldn't be, he told himself. The near-est women were in mining camps twenty to thirty miles east of where he was.

The humming grew louder. Through the trees across the clearing a human form flitted. Fargo could not quite believe his eyes. It was a woman, sure enough, dressed in clothes as white as the snow, skipping along as if she were taking a merry stroll through a city park. In her right hand she swung something large back and forth.

Totally bewildered, Fargo veered to intercept her. There was a chance she had seen the Ovaro. Then, too, he needed to warn her about the wildman. His footfalls were muffled by the heavy snow, so he was almost on top of her before she sensed another presence and turned.

Fargo stopped, smiling to demonstrate that he was friendly. "Don't be afraid," he said. It did not help.

The woman took one look at him and the revolver he clasped, and lit out of there as if her heels were on fire. She did not cry out or scream, though, which in itself was odd.

"Wait!" Fargo hollered, to no avail. She fled like a frightened doe, threading through the trees with a skill that hinted at long experience in the wild. He sped after her, tantalized by the glimpse he'd had of wavy raven hair framed by an ermine hood and an alluring face as milky and smooth as the finest cream.

When the woman had turned, Fargo recognized the object she held. Like the wildman and the woman herself, it was out of place, bizarre. The sight of it was almost enough to convince him that the woman must be a fragment of his overworked imagination.

Here he was, in the middle of nowhere with a snowstorm fading rapidly around him, and what should he stumble on but a beautiful woman in a white fur coat, traipsing through the forest *with a picnic basket* in her hand!

"Wait!" Fargo called again, struggling to keep the vision of loveliness in view. Her white coat blended so perfectly into the white background that if not for the brown basket, she would have been invisible. Several times she cast petrified glances over her slender shoulder.

"I won't hurt you!" Fargo called out. He should have saved his breath. She kept on fleeing, a pale ghost among ghostly trees, leaving tracks that were uncommonly shallow, almost as if she spurned the ground in her flight.

The snowfall had abated even more. In the storm's wake the mountains had been transformed into a pristine, hoary wonderland. A thick white shroud covered everything. It layered branches in frosty white. It mantled brush in chalky hues. Logs were white bumps on the forest floor. Boulders had dandruff.

It occurred to Fargo that the woman was gradually looping her way back to the general area where he had spotted her. The insight spurred him into cutting through a grassy belt to head her off. She did not notice. Intent on eluding him, she did not awaken to his ploy until he crashed through high weeds beside her and grasped her wrist.

"No!" the woman wailed, jerking and tugging in a frenzy. "Let go of me!"

"I only want to warn you—" Fargo said, but got no further. In desperation the woman swung the picnic basket at his head. He ducked a shade slow. It clipped him on the temple hard enough to buckle his legs. Pain seared his skull, and his vision spun.

The woman tore loose. A thud heralded her flight. Fargo, shaking his head to clear it, pushed to his feet just as a thicket closed around her fur-bundled form. He took a faltering stride, intending to chase her however far it took to bring her to bay, when something snagged his right foot, tripping him. He went to one knee.

Assuming that a log or boulder was to blame, Fargo began to rise once more. He changed his mind when he discovered that the object he had fallen over was her picnic basket. She had flung it aside so she would not be burdened by the extra weight.

Fargo holstered his pistol. Enough was enough. The woman had made it plain that she wanted nothing to do with him. So be it. He'd go find the stallion and continue his trek eastward.

First, though, Fargo opened the basket, not knowing what to expect. But what else would a picnic basket contain? Food galore had been packed to the brim. Salted strips of beef, fragrant cheeses, canned goods, crackers, and more, all had been neatly arranged to make the most of the limited space.

His mouth watered, his stomach rumbled. Two days had gone by since he ate last, and he was famished. Fargo scanned the woods but saw no trace of the woman. She might object to his helping himself, but after what she had done, he felt that he deserved to. After all, he had only been trying to warn her about the man who tried to kill him a while ago. She had no call to turn on him as she had done.

The beef proved too tantalizing to resist. Fargo bit off a sizable chunk, smacking his lips at the delicious flavor. A few mouthfuls convinced him that it was the tastiest, juiciest jerky he had ever eaten, and that said a lot.

Standing, Fargo walked westward, chewing lustily. Clouds rolled by overhead, but the snow had about ended, the wind had died. No one could sneak up on him any longer. He would be safe so long as he stuck to open ground.

His hunger merely whetted, Fargo regarded the assortment of cheeses with interest. It would serve the woman right, he reflected, if he finished off every last morsel. Plucking out a yellowish-green wedge that stank to high heaven, he bit half off. It tasted a lot better than it smelled. A brown wedge had a spicy taste. A third was soft and mushy.

The forest had thinned to scattered stands of pines. The woman was nowhere to be seen, but Fargo had a hunch that she was close by, spying on him.

Cramming salted crackers into his mouth, the big man made for a rise that overlooked the eastern half of the table-land. The food had made him thirsty enough to drain a river. So he was delighted when he lifted a packet of meat and found a full whiskey bottle lying on its side.

Beaming, Fargo came to the top of the rise and set the basket down. Whoever that woman had been, she knew the way to a man's heart! Eagerly he opened the heaven-sent gift. Straightening, he tipped the whiskey to his mouth but never swallowed. For as his gaze roved beyond the rise, he went rigid with amazement and questioned his sanity.

A stone's throw away reared the structure he had seen from afar. It had no business being there, yet it was undeniably real. As alien as the wildman and the woman in white, before him sprawled an enormous brooding castle.